# 1,000,000 Books
are available to read at

www.ForgottenBooks.com

Read online
Download PDF
Purchase in print

ISBN 978-1-331-44620-0
PIBN 10191292

This book is a reproduction of an important historical work. Forgotten Books uses state-of-the-art technology to digitally reconstruct the work, preserving the original format whilst repairing imperfections present in the aged copy. In rare cases, an imperfection in the original, such as a blemish or missing page, may be replicated in our edition. We do, however, repair the vast majority of imperfections successfully; any imperfections that remain are intentionally left to preserve the state of such historical works.

Forgotten Books is a registered trademark of FB &c Ltd.
Copyright © 2018 FB &c Ltd.
FB &c Ltd, Dalton House, 60 Windsor Avenue, London, SW19 2RR.
Company number 08720141. Registered in England and Wales.

For support please visit www.forgottenbooks.com

# 1 MONTH OF FREE READING

## at
## www.ForgottenBooks.com

By purchasing this book you are eligible for one month membership to ForgottenBooks.com, giving you unlimited access to our entire collection of over 1,000,000 titles via our web site and mobile apps.

To claim your free month visit:
www.forgottenbooks.com/free191292

\* Offer is valid for 45 days from date of purchase. Terms and conditions apply.

English
Français
Deutsche
Italiano
Español
Português

# www.forgottenbooks.com

**Mythology** Photography **Fiction**
Fishing Christianity **Art** Cooking
Essays Buddhism Freemasonry
Medicine **Biology** Music **Ancient Egypt** Evolution Carpentry Physics
Dance Geology **Mathematics** Fitness
Shakespeare **Folklore** Yoga Marketing
**Confidence** Immortality Biographies
Poetry **Psychology** Witchcraft
Electronics Chemistry History **Law**
Accounting **Philosophy** Anthropology
Alchemy Drama Quantum Mechanics
Atheism Sexual Health **Ancient History**
**Entrepreneurship** Languages Sport
Paleontology Needlework Islam
**Metaphysics** Investment Archaeology
Parenting Statistics Criminology
**Motivational**

# ADAM AND EVE.

BY THE AUTHOR OF
'DOROTHY FOX,' AND 'THE PRESCOTTS OF PAMPHILLON.'

IN THREE VOLUMES.
VOL. I.

LONDON:
RICHARD BENTLEY AND SON,
Publishers in Ordinary to Her Majesty the Queen.

# ADAM AND EVE.

## CHAPTER I.

TOWARDS the close of a July evening, in the upper room of a house, which stood in one of London's narrowest thoroughfares, a woman sat striving to penetrate the tangled perplexities of her future.

Her hands were idle; her eyes rested on a low chair with a rail back and a patch-work cushion, her mother's chair, in which she had been wont to see a tender face and frail, bent figure; but now in place of that loved form there rose before her a solitary mound of newly-turned earth; and a sense of her utter desolation sweeping over her, Eve Pascal flung herself down in an agony of tears, and let the torrent of her grief run dry.

Then she arose, stretching out her arms as if in mute entreaty to some invisible presence, and took a step nearer the window, straining her eyes to catch sight of the sky, the very light of which was obscured and blotted out by the mass of chimneys from warehouses and workshops.

From the window, Eve let her gaze wander round the small room, inconveniently filled with heavy furniture, treasured by her mother as bearing testimony to former thrift and respectable belongings, for Mrs. Pascal had come of a family who had seen better days, in right of which they could never overlook that their orphan cousin had thrown herself away on a common seafaring man who had nothing but his handsome face and his dare-devil stories to set before her; and although the despised husband never returned from the voyage, during which Eve was born, the relations saw in this no cause to restrain their tongues nor alter their judgment, and the sore-hearted widow, resenting these continual jobations, gradually withdrew herself from her family, until not only had all communication ceased between them, but their very existence was no longer known to her.

As Eve's gaze fell successively on a tall eight-day clock, with a brass-bound chest of drawers on one side, and a corresponding but more bulky set on the other, she gave an audible sigh.

'You'll try and keep the furniture together, Eve?' her mother had said.

And Eve had promptly answered, 'Yes,' in that spirit which then forbade her to think of gainsaying the slightest request which Mrs. Pascal might make; the same spirit still filled the girl's heart, but her mind was troubled, and her thoughts oppressed, by the narrow loneliness of the life which, if she remained here, she saw spread out before her.

Mrs. Pascal had supported herself by clear-starching and fine-mending;

she had taught her daughter enough to enable her to gain a living by the same employment, but up to the time of her mother's illness, although never refusing her assistance, Eve had not taken kindly to needlework. No sooner, however, did she feel that the responsibility of providing for her mother's comfort depended on her exertions, than she sat down with the most willing alacrity, and managed the little business so deftly and so well, that a great load was lifted from the widow's heart, and she rested assured that she might lay aside all anxiety on the score of her child's future daily bread.

But the work which had been a pleasure then, had become an irksome labour now; the monotony of the quiet employment was unendurable. Death had snapped asunder the bondage to which love had submitted, and, without any power to oppose it, the girl's nature asserted itself and refused to continue longer its course of uneventful existence. Up to the morning of the previous day, these longings and yearnings after freedom had been hopeless, but an unlooked-for letter had changed the whole current of events, and had sent her pent-up thoughts and wishes hurrying off through a thousand new and unexplored channels.

This letter had come from her uncle, her father's half-brother, in answer to a letter she had sent announcing her mother's death. Eve had written this letter in compliance with her mother's request—a request made because it had seemed, to Mrs. Pascal's mind, a respect due to her husband's memory that his family should be told of her death, and thereby know that there was one the less to bear their name.

Beyond the fact that her husband had a brother and some cousins living in an out-of-the-way village in Cornwall, Mrs. Pascal knew nothing of these relations. She had written to them when the news of Andrew's death came, telling them that she was left with one child, a girl; and had received a reply that if 'she'd come down and live among them, they'd do for her and the little maid.' But the stories which her husband had told of his native village, and the life lived there, had filled the town-bred wife with horror; and, though she thanked them for their kind offer, she felt she would sooner beg her bread in London than live at ease with those, who, to use her husband's words, 'feared neither God nor devil.'

Since this letter, no further communication had passed between them; and when Eve had written her sad announcement, it was with a strong feeling that in all probability this uncle was long ago dead, and that (only she had given her mother the promise) she might well spare herself the trouble of sending the letter.

A fortnight passed by, and now an answer had come, couched in very much the same words, and containing an offer very similar to that which, some twenty years before, Mrs. Pascal had refused: namely, that if Eve would come and see them, they would make her welcome for as long as she liked to stay.

As Eve read this letter, her face

flushed with excitement; for a time the burden of her grief was lifted off her heart, and her quick imagination carried her at once to the far-off village where 'the houses were washed by the waves, the rocks rose high as mountains, and you could stand at your door and see the great ships sail by.'

Eve's pulse quickened at the picture, for she was a sailor's child, and her inheritance was the love that is born in the hearts of those whose fathers, and their fathers before them, have gone down to the sea in ships, and seen the wonders of the deep.

Mrs. Pascal's recollections of the stories her husband had told, had been unwittingly kept alive by the interest his daughter took in them. The storms, the wrecks, the tales of hair-breadth escapes, and of drowned men, which made the mother's heart beat with fear, filled Eve with excitement, and wonder that her father should have left that life for such dull security as they possessed.

It never occurred to her to propose that her mother should leave London; such a thing would have seemed not only improbable, but impossible. In those days, unless some great event befell them, people lived and died where they were born; necessity was the only recognised obligation for leaving one place to go to another, and any desire to roam was looked upon as the offspring of an ill-regulated disposition. Therefore it was only at such moments as these that Eve gave expression to the wish which leavened her inmost thoughts, and coloured with romance her idle dreams—to go out into the world, to see people she had never seen before, to live some life other than the daily routine of dull respectability, to have joys and sorrows springing out of unforeseen accidents and strange emergencies, to be the centre of hopes and fears. These and a hundred more extravagant longings had lain smouldering in Eve's breast, to be set ablaze by this letter, which seemed to open out the way leading to the new existence after which she so greedily thirsted. There was but one drawback, and that was the knowledge that, in accepting her uncle's offer, she would be acting in direct opposition to her mother's wishes—not her expressed wishes—for the possibility of such an offer had never occurred to Mrs. Pascal's mind; although, had it done so, she would have felt perfectly secure that Eve would never entertain the thought of leaving the place where she had been brought up and had friends, to live dependent upon relations whose ways were more in keeping with the godless heathens than the repectable people of a Christian country.

But Eve well knew that, if her mother were alive, she would never have ventured to propose the step she now contemplated, and this fact alone was weighty enough to set the balance trembling between this and her future happiness.

'What could I do with the furniture?' she said, with a despondent movement of her hands.

'Perhaps Reuben would take care of it,' suggested that temporising spirit always at hand when battle wages between duty and inclination. 'You need only go for a time,' insinuated the tempter; 'and the room behind his shop is always empty.'

Eve frowned; she admitted the suggestion, but disliked the expedient, feeling she had no right to ask a favour from a man who needed but encouragement to ask, on his part, a boon which she could never grant. But the tare of desire was already springing up, choking the resolutions she had so recently made; and before another hour passed by, Eve was resolved to write and tell her uncle that she accepted his offer, for a time at least, and that she would start for Polperro as soon as she had safely housed, with a friend, the furniture which her mother had bidden her keep. Then she took out her hat, and prepared to get ready to go on an errand which would take her through the street, at the far end of which was a small shop, bearing over it the name of 'Reuben May, Watch and Clockmaker.'

## CHAPTER II.

THE owner of this shop, Reuben May, was a young man rather below the middle size, with a thin, spare figure and an earnest, thoughtful face; his complexion was sallow, and his features by no means good, except his forehead which was broad and well shaped, and his eyes which were bright and penetrating.

From boyhood Reuben had shown a sober, studious disposition, and to this, as he grew older, he added an independence of thought and opinion which attracted him towards the then fast-increasing body of Methodists. It was through this common bond of religious opinion that Reuben's acquaintance with Mrs. Pascal had been brought about. They had fallen into speaking and hand-shaking through sitting near to each other in the little chapel which both frequented; this had led to walking home together, discussing the sermon and the minister, until, from a certain sympathy of thought and opinion, a feeling of friendship sprung up between them, and Mrs. Pascal, seeing that the young fellow had no relations and few, if any, friends, had invited him to come to her house, an invitation which Reuben readily accepted, and had so completely benefited by that at the time of her death, next to her daughter, the chief mourner at the widow's humble grave had been Reuben May.

When, from necessity, Eve was obliged to carry home her work, Reuben would often take her place by the sick woman's bed, and at such times open his heart with a frankness he had never before shown; tell her of his aspirations, his failings, and his weaknesses, the strongest of which he confessed, with some shamefacedness, to be an overpowering love for her daughter Eve, which, in spite of scanty encouragement and small hope of return, he found himself unable to overcome.

Poor Mrs. Pascal! it was no slight task to withhold herself from giving some small encouragement to the furtherance of a union, the accomplishment of which had been one of the fondest desires of her heart. For months her eyes had never fallen on these two without the wish coming that their lives might be united in marriage; but the nearer she approached that time when all earthly interests must be given up, the firmer grew her conviction that this wish of her heart had best be abandoned. Feeling sore at the disappointment, she had on almost the last occasion of these confidences told Reuben, that many a time she had had it in her mind to chide him for not having more cunning in his speech to Eve; and Reuben had regretfully acknowledged the too frequent sharpness of a tongue very prone to give offence, for, unluckily for the success of Reuben's suit, his love had eyes, and his religion was in that stage when zeal is apt to run ahead of discretion.

Did but the suspicion of a shadow come into her mother's face, and Eve's quick retort or stinging repartee was swallowed down and repented of; but she desired that her words should be as thorns and nettles to Reuben's outspoken censures and rebukes; and if she could but discover she was causing a smart, fresh fuel was added to the fire of her tongue. And yet, knowing this, seeing her motive, and wincing under her utter disregard of his annoyance, Eve was dearer to him than all the world; his heart craved after her love, and lay as a stone within him in presence of any other woman.

As he sat on this June evening close up to the small window, apparently engrossed in repairing the cog-wheel of the watch he held in his hand, any one might have said, there was a man very far removed from the rose-tinted region of romance. Yet the God-sent gift of love had been lodged within his breast, and was spreading its halo over all he saw and did.

Mechanically he turned over his tools and found the one best suited to his work; but even while he did so, he was looking on a vision in which his heart was no longer solitary, neither was his lot lonely. Hand in hand he and his elect walked through life, and lo! earth with its toilsome roads and cloudy skies became paradise; and as he still dreamed on, a voice close by awakened him, and, looking up, the Eve of this Eden stood before him.

'Why, Reuben, you seemed scared,' she said, smiling at the dazed look on the young man's face.

'And no wonder,' he replied, quickly recovering himself, 'for I do believe this is the first time you've ever put foot inside my place!'

'I wanted to have a little talk with you,' said Eve, ignoring the slight reproach which Reuben's words were meant to convey; 'and I thought, as I had to go out, I'd come round by here and ask you if you'd much to do this evening?'

'Nothing that'll hinder anything you may want of me,' returned Reuben, promptly; 'the light's all but gone, and, anyway, I should have been thinking of shutting up in the course of a half hour or so. Could you step inside for the value of ten minutes?' he asked, lifting up the portion of the counter which covered the entrance partition.

To his surprise Eve stepped through, and, Reuben having cleared a chair, she seated herself, while he returned to what was, after this, but a mere pretence of finishing his work.

'You've a nice-sized room here,' observed Eve, taking a critical survey of the apartment.

'Fairish,' said Reuben, endeavouring to keep under the thumping of his heart, which rendered ordinary conversation somewhat trying.

'It would take plenty more than you've got in it now?' continued Eve, interrogatively.

'Oh yes! no doubt but it would hold a thing or two more,' said Reuben, very fierce with himself for being put out of countenance by this slim young thing, who could look at him and his belongings with the most enviable composure.

He would not allow himself to be

mastered; it was against all reason that he, Reuben May, who could hold his own, ah! and better than his own, with most men he knew, should be set trembling like an aspen leaf because of a pale face and a pair of grey eyes; the thing was ridiculous, and, to prove it, he took up one tool after another, examining them critically, and whistling the while with an air of the most abstracted unconcern.

An expression of vexation, then of disappointment, passed over Eve's face; that was not the way men took love. Surely Reuben could not care for her so much as she had counted upon, or he would never sit whistling there, and she close by.

Although not favourably disposed towards the lover, Eve coveted the love; she wanted to see some one racked with torture, driven to despair, called into life by a smile, and killed by a frown. This was love read by the index of her own passionate nature, for Eve had nothing else to teach her; she knew no experience, no books to tell her how many a strange disguise the blind god walks under. As she felt, Reuben ought to feel, that is, if he loved her; and if not, then came the temptation to make him, and this impulse made her throw a touch of sadness into her voice as she said :

'In spite of what you say, Reuben, I see that you are busy to-night, and I mustn't expect that you are going to give up your time to me whenever I may want any little thing of you; but, you see, I haven't got anybody, as it were, to go to— not now.'

But before the 'now' came trembling

out, Reuben had recklessly swept away all his tools, had jumped up, pushed back his chair, and was making a dash towards the outer place where he kept the shutters.

'I won't be a minute, Eve,' he said. 'I haven't got nothing to do, indeed I haven't; and then I shall be ready to go anywhere, wherever you like, with you. I ain't busy a bit; I wasn't doing anything; I was only thinking—of—something.'

Eve gave a reassured smile, and then, seeing he was pausing to know her wishes, she said:

'I do want to have a talk with you, and I thought, if you wouldn't mind it, we might go to Holloway, and then I could speak to you as we went along.'

Reuben gave a ready acquiescence, and only detaining Eve while he smartened-up his appearance in keeping with the honour of the occasion, they started off for St. Mark's churchyard, in a corner of which was Mrs. Pascal's humble grave. Engrossed by the separate interests which filled their minds, they had gone a considerable distance without a word being exchanged between them. Suddenly Reuben awoke to this fact, and, doubtful how his companion might be affected by it, he cast a somewhat disturbed glance in her direction; but, instead of displeasure, he was reassured with a smile, which accepting as a good omen, he resolved to turn to immediate account, and at once made a desperate plunge by saying:

'Love's a queer sort of a thing, Eve, isn't it?'

'Queer?' she said, with a surprised look; 'how queer, Reuben?'

'Why, in its ways it is. It comes to

you whether you will or not, and it settles on the one it makes choice of, no matter what you have to say for or against it.'

'Oh, I don't think that would ever be your case;' and Eve pursed up her lips and gave a decided shake of her head. 'You always tell me that every right-minded person acts from principle, and has no doubt about choosing right from wrong; and of course you speak from experience.'

Reuben tried to waive the thrust by saying :

'That's a very good rule, but, you know, every rule has an exception;' and he gave a sigh, as he looked towards her, which seemed to say the exception in his case had come now. 'Only you just look here, now,' he said, after a few minutes spent in silent debate as to the best mode of entering upon the difficulties of his subject; 'supposing I was to set you to pick out among all the young women you see—say at chapel, then—the one you thought was best fitted to be my wife, what's the sort of one you'd fix upon, eh? Come, give me your idea of the right sort of woman for me to take!'

'Oh, I know exactly,' returned Eve promptly, conjuring up a vision of a certain Tamson Walters, whose propriety and decorum had often been held up to her as a model which she might fitly follow. 'She ought to be short and square, with a little fat face, and light-blue eyes, and her mouth ought to be buttoned-up so, and her nose turned up like that.'

'Come, never mind her looks,' laughed Reuben, forced into recognising the intended caricature. 'When a man's got matrimony in his eye, he mustn't only look skin-deep; if he does, he deserves the doll he's sure to get.'

'Oh, but wait, I'm going on to the rest,' for Eve was anxious to do justice to her rival's peculiarities. 'Only you must let me draw her my own way, you know. I'm always obliged to describe the outside as well as the inside of a person I want other people to see. Of course she must have experienced *conversion*, and so be able to rebuke those whose hearts are still dwelling in sin, which is certain to be the case if they don't push back all their hair, and hide it, like she does, under a hideous net cap with no border.'

Reuben gave a reproving shake of his head.

'Come, that'll do,' he said; 'I know who you're pointing to, and all I say is, I wish all women were made out of such good stuff as Tamson Walters is. The man who calls her wife, I shall call a lucky chap.'

'Then why don't you let that man be yourself?' said Eve. 'I'm sure, if you ask her, she couldn't say less than "Verily I will" to her *dear* brother Reuben.'

And the manner of her mimicry, as she folded her hands and let drop her eyes, was so bewitching, that all the reproof Reuben had ready to say died on his lips; and looking at her with eyes which told his tale far more eloquently than words, he said:

'But suppose I don't want her to say "yes." Suppose I'm foolish enough to set my heart on somebody who can tease me into a rage one minute, and set me in a good temper the next—who one hour I say I never want to see any more, and the next I'm counting the minutes that'll bring the time when we'll meet again—who worries and torments me so, that do what I can, I can't get her out of my head by night nor day—who's got more faults than anybody I ever knew, and yet if I was asked how I'd have her altered, I could not tell you, for the life of me. Ah, Eve, you may well laugh!' he exclaimed, reflecting the smile which had overspread her face; 'for if I was to talk from now to next week, I could never make you know the great fool you've made and are still making of me.'

'I?' the smile turned into an expression of the most bewildered astonishment; 'why, what have I got to do with it, Reuben?'

'What have you got to do with it? as if you didn't know all the time I was talking about you—that's just one of your teasing ways; why, the minute I began you knew what was sticking in my throat and wouldn't come out. You've known for twelve months and more what I've been wanting to say, only that I saw the foolishness of it; and, as far as that goes, I see it still, but I can't get over it. Oh, Eve! you're as the very apple of my eye!' he said, with increasing earnestness. 'Sometimes I think it must be the allurements of the devil, and then I'm for putting it down to the workings of the Almighty; anyway, all I know is, I can't battle against it any longer—it's mastered me altogether; and though I promised your mother I'd act by you like a brother, and put aside all the rest, I can't do it,

Eve, that I can't. Unless you'll promise to settle down into trying to make up your mind to marry me, I must go away far off from here to some place where I shan't see nor hear of you again.'

Eve's heart leaped up in triumph. He did love her then, and in spite of himself, too. This man, who was always teaching and reproving, and trying to be her master, was after all her slave. For a moment every other feeling was swallowed up in victory—but only for a moment—for pity was already near, and in another instant was clamouring so loud that Eve had to ask its name before she could assure herself the voice she heard was not the subtle voice of love.

'Oh, Reuben!' she said, 'why didn't you tell me all this before?'

'I thought you knew it,' he said.

'No, I didn't quite know it. I used to think sometimes that you cared a little; and then something would come and I'd think you didn't. Of course I saw you liked to talk to me and that—but I didn't know that what you felt was real love!'

'Real love?' he echoed. 'What do women know about real love? A little dribbling fondness for somebody who can make them pretty speeches, that's all they feel. While I—I've wrestled with love as 'twere a giant, and the giant has thrown me so that I lie on the ground helpless, and whether 'tis best to hope for life or death from you, God knows—I don't!'

And he stood for a few moments all but mastered by his emotion. A little sigh escaped Eve, and the sound seemed to arouse Reuben, and bring him back to the present.

'Mine's a queer kind of courting, Eve,' he said, looking up and meeting her troubled face. 'I know I ain't saying a bit what I ought to, to you, but for all that I've got it in my heart to try to make you comfortable; and you should have all I could give you, and not more to do than you'd a mind to do. As far as I could make it, your life should go easy with you, Eve.'

'Easy with me?' she cried contemptuously; 'as if I cared for sitting still all my life—doing nothing, seeing nothing, being nothing!'

'It ain't a bad sort of life though, Eve. I don't see that a woman wants much more.'

'Oh, don't you! But there, it's no good you and me beginning to argue, Reuben; or I should say I don't see how a man can want so little as to sit indoors all day over the mending of a few clocks and watches. Oh, if I'd been a man, do you think I'd have been contented to be nothing more than a clockmaker?'

'Who says I'm contented to be nothing but a clockmaker?' said Reuben, quickly. ''Tisn't because I'm not one of your bloodthirsty chaps with a nose for powder and an eye always cocked for seeing daylight through my fellow-creatures, that I'm contented to sit quiet by and see the world go round me. I often believe that if it wasn't for you, Eve, I should have turned my mind on something else long before this.'

'Do you?' she said, with surprise. 'Why, what else could you do, Reuben?'

'What else could I do?' he repeated. 'Well, a good many things that I don't think small of, though I don't suppose any would make me cut a much better figure in your eyes.'

For a minute Eve did not answer, then she said:

'I've been thinking whether I couldn't be of some use to somebody. I've heard dear mother tell of women who have worked wonders, and done good among people who wouldn't hear a word from a man.'

'Ah, they were women of your mother's sort, though,' said Reuben, seizing on this opportunity for retaliation. 'You ain't a bit like her in any way.'

'Of course, I know I'm not half so good,' said Eve, not over-pleased with this candour, 'nor never shall be.'

'Never!' said Reuben, decisively. 'So it wouldn't be of any use your trying anything of that sort. You might be seeming to convert a man so long as he had some hopes of marrying you, but,' he added, 'take my word for it, it wouldn't last longer than that.'

'Oh, I know you've a very poor opinion of what women can do,' said Eve.

'No, I haven't,' replied Reuben; 'that is, so long as they do well what they were ordained for—sitting in their own houses mending the clothes, and tending the children.'

And he gave a little inward chuckle over the nettle he was proving himself to Eve.

For a moment Eve was bent on finding an equally smart retort, but a sudden thought told her that she held a sharper weapon to pierce Reuben with, than the mere bandying of words could be. So, affecting her most placid smile, she said blandly:

'Thank you, Reuben, for showing me the life your wife will have to lead. I'm much obliged for the offer, but you'll excuse me saying that the situation wouldn't suit me.'

'Oh, very well,' said Reuben, trying to smother his love, in his vexation with himself and his anger against her; 'then my course is chalked out for me very clear. Off I go—the farther away the better—to some place where I can't ever see or hear of you again.'

And as he jerked out the words, he involuntarily turned to see how such an appalling announcement was affecting her. Not very much, apparently, for the smile had become more triumphant, as, seizing the opportunity, she pointed her sharpest arrow by saying :

'Please don't do anything rash on my account, particularly as there's no need for it, for the thing I had to tell you was that I'm going away myself. My uncle in Cornwall has written up for me to go down there and live with him among my father's people.'

'But you won't go?' exclaimed Reuben, forgetting all his own lately-vaunted resolutions.

'Why shouldn't I go?' said Eve. 'I've nothing nor nobody to keep me where I am.'

'But,' said Reuben, 'haven't you heard your mother speak of them as a wild rough lot who she shuddered to think of? Nonsense, Eve, what would a girl like you do amongst such a set as you'd find there?'

'Do? A great deal of good, perhaps; and if not,' she added, seeing the look which came into Reuben's face, 'what harm could they do me?'

'What harm could they do you?' he repeated slowly. 'Why, Eve, surely you know that next to doing bad deeds yourself, comes the lending countenance to them who do them. As I heard Howell Harris say, "As well eat the devil, as the broth he's boiled in."'

'I've only promised to go down and see them,' said Eve, somewhat disturbed by Reuben's plain speaking. 'I needn't stay more than a year, unless I like. Come,' she continued, seeking reassurance, 'there can't much harm happen in a year, Reuben?'

'More than you think,' he replied gravely.

Then, after standing for a minute silent, he burst out with:

'A whole year?—never to see you—speak to you—know where you are, or what you're turning to?—oh! it's cruel—cruel! Why should Providence deal so hard with me? What have I ever done that all my heart should be set like this upon one who doesn't care a brass button for its love or its hate?'

The tone of these words, and the look of anguish Reuben's face wore as he spoke them, touched Eve's, and she said:

'Oh, Reuben, don't say that; it isn't kind—after all you've done for me, too. I do care for you very much, but how was I to know what you felt? Why didn't you speak to me like this before? Then,

I don't know, it might have been different; but instead of that you've always spoken to me so off-hand-like, that I thought you fancied love was a thing to be ashamed of.'

'Well, and so my love did make me ashamed,' returned Reuben, fiercely; 'and well it might, when I saw it was only made a laughing-stock and a jeer of. Why, haven't I seen you turn up your nose if by chance I so much as mentioned the word love?'

The colour came up into Eve's face, and, with a little confusion, she answered:

'Indeed, Reuben, if I seemed to do that, 'twas only pretending, and for fear you should guess some of the silly thoughts I have in my head when I sit romancing.'

'Oh, hang romancing!' exclaimed Reuben, pettishly; 'it's death and destruction to truth and commonplace sober reality. Life's too short, and time's too precious, to be spent in picturing up a pack of beaux and dandies that——'

'Oh, you don't understand me, Reuben,' said Eve, hopelessly.

'No, nor I never shall while you're up there in the clouds; though sometimes I think '—and he turned on her face a look saddened, yet full of admiration—'that it's the most fitting place for such an angel as you seem to me.'

'Who's romancing now, I should like to know?' exclaimed Eve, her vanity touched by Reuben's rarely acknowledged tribute to her good looks.

'Why me, of course! Oh, you've but to pull the right string, and your puppet will dance to whatever tune you choose to play. Though, so far as romance goes, 'tis an old chum of mine, and until thinking of you drove out all chance of thinking of anything else from my precious head, has helped me to get through many a dull day.'

Eve gave a little smile of amused content; she had never before so much enjoyed a walk with Reuben. Her tickled vanity set her pity in motion, and she began to feel so much compassion that it made her quite sorry to think she was going away from him. It seemed, too, so hard to crush all this despair—to take away from him all plea for suffering any more.

What could she do to adjust matters to a better balance? Ask him to wait? Tell him she would give him his answer at the end of the year when she came back? Acting on this suggestion, Eve spoke at once, fearing, if she hesitated, that the whisper of a conscience which disapproved this action would make itself heard, and she should be forced into being honest, and obliged to give Reuben now his final 'No.'

Therefore it happened that when they parted that evening, an understanding had been entered into between them, that, though there was no engagement on either part, each was bound, in case of change, to render an account of his or her feelings to the other.

## CHAPTER III.

NOW, under ordinary circumstances, and once secure that he possessed her love, Reuben would have willingly served his seven years for Eve, feeling a certain satisfaction that there was to be a period of probation, during which time he should be able to regain that mastery over himself which this present all-absorbing state of love seemed to have completely wrested from his grasp.

Reuben prided himself on his calm unemotional temperament, and it chafed him not a little to find his nature subverted and his volition destroyed because of a fair face whose smile or frown made his joy or sorrow. His reason yet remained sufficiently independent, and often in his calmer moments the conviction was still forced upon him that, seeing how widely Eve's principles and opinions differed from his own, his sensibility ought to have continued subservient to his judgment, and, until he had convinced her that her way of viewing things was false, and her arguments unsound, he ought never to have urged her to become the partner of his home.

Disputation was Reuben's forte, and it was a matter of great wonderment to many why he did not give up his business, which was not over successful, and adopt the vocation of a lay preacher, for which he seemed so evidently suited.

Reuben often dwelt upon this possibility himself, and was somewhat surprised that he should feel so lukewarm towards a calling, which in others had for him many attractions; but the secret of his indifference, perhaps, lay in this fact, that for him to be a preacher seemed an easy matter, a thing at hand to be taken up any day, while the business by which he earned his daily bread had not, so far, proved a happy choice. If he gave it up, Fate, Providence, or whatever name we give to the power which orders the everyday events of our life, would have proved too strong for him, and he would have to confess himself defeated, and defeat of any kind was most unpalatable to Reuben May; indeed, so far as his personal concerns went, it was a word to which he would give no meaning; he had no tolerance for failure, and no pity for those who failed. Why should people fail? he had never failed, and nobody had ever helped him. Both his parents had died when he was a boy, leaving him to shift for himself, and so good a shift had he made that, since that time, he had, unaided and alone, supported himself, taught himself, apprenticed himself, and had finally, by his own exertions, scraped together the small sum needed to open his little shop with.

His argument was, that what others had done he could do, and what he had done others could do; a reasoning which outsteps vanity to fix its standard on self-approbation.

The magnet which attracted and drew together the sympathies of Reuben and

Eve was, that within the nature of each lay a vein of enthusiasm and aspiration which carried them beyond the daily round of their everyday lives. Both had strong wills, fervid temperaments, and vivid imaginations, more or less warped by the cramping influence from which they suffered, in being constantly surrounded by a narrow sphere of persons, who looked on all that lay beyond the grasp of their own stunted reasons as something reprehensible and not respectable.

Even Mrs. Pascal, good, worthy woman as she was, had not entirely escaped this bias; and when, at times, Eve would open wide her heart and speak from out its fulness, the mother would be troubled at her child's strange fancies, and would cast about to find where the mistake lay in her bringing up, that she had turned out so widely different from those models after whom she would fain have fashioned her speech and her thoughts, as she had to her utmost done her cap and her gown.

Reuben, too, knowing that he had never been able to get up the slightest interest in those demure virgins from amid whose ranks his choice should necessarily have fallen, revenged himself by chiming in with Mrs. Pascal, praising their sedate appearance and demure behaviour, and ignoring the fact that in external propriety, at least, Eve differed but very little from the rest of the young women among whom, at chapel or meeting, she was seated.

Mrs. Pascal's naturally shy, retiring disposition had been against her making many friends; and as—though a constant attendant at the chapel—she had never summoned up enough resolution to become a member until her illness, though known to all the congregation by sight, and sufficiently intimate with most of them to exchange hand-shakings, but very few had ever seen her in her own home.

As soon, however, as it became known that she was dangerously ill, she was the object of constant and unremitting attentions, and scarce a day passed without a visit from one or other of her friends.

But the conversation which soothed and calmed the weary spirit of the sick woman was torture to poor Eve; the hope raised of that bright world unseen fell like a funeral knell upon her ears; the glories of that land beyond the grave, to which her mother now was hastening, she would not listen to, because her eyes were fixed upon the grave itself, and the great desolation she saw there blotted all else beyond from out her view.

Looking from the level of declining middle age, good, worthy people, as these were, no longer see the whirlwinds which scatter and destroy youth's golden sands; their blood grown torpid, their affections lukewarm, they fail to recognise the throes which usher in the birth of calm endurance.

When Eve, in the strength of her passionate love, wrestled with the dread enemy whose shadow already rested on her mother's face, they called it presumption; and when, seeing his visible presence draw near, the girl, in the helpless agony of mute despair, threw up her arms to—if but for an instant—avert the fatal dart, the action was denounced as an implied defiance of Almighty Will. Misapplied rebukes, untimely reasoning, and comfortless platitudes were showered on her to no purpose: 'Leave me alone, only leave me alone!' she would moan to those who had left their work or their pleasure for the sole purpose of carrying out the good that in their hearts they constantly desired to do. It was neither their fault nor hers that they could not understand her, and she could not tolerate them; yet the breach produced scandal on one side, and vexation and disquietude on both.

It was during this time that the chord between Reuben and Eve had first truly vibrated; Reuben's sympathy was as dumb as Eve's sorrow, and because he sat silently by, neither attempting to console her anguish nor curb its outbreak, his was the only presence she could tolerate

But this preference shown, and shown for a man too, was but a further aggravation of Eve's already numerous offences. Neither did Reuben May, although a favourite, altogether escape his share of censure; but though Reuben was pretty certain of the animadversions he was bringing down upon himself, they in no way influenced his conduct, for, added to the attraction which Eve possessed for him, the affection in which he had held Mrs. Pascal had been all but filial, and in itself had prompted him to watch over each trifling detail of the humble funeral, which Eve had entrusted to his care; and when the poor girl found strength to thank him for his solicitude, finding some comfort in the thought that all was carried out as her mother would have desired, Reuben was doubly repaid for the trouble he had taken, and the small hoard of savings which, on his own part, he had expended.

A novice in the ways of love, Reuben did not know that one of the surest tests of the strength of his lay in the fact, that never at any former moment, when her beauty had been most radiant and her spirits most brilliant, had Eve seemed half so dear to his heart as she was during those dark days of sorrow when, with swollen eyes and tear-stained face, she sat unmindful of his presence, hardly heeding when he came or when he went. He forgot then all the vanity for which he used to chide her, all the inconsistencies for which he had been wont to condemn her; he only felt that if she would remain helpless all her days so that he might wait upon her and work for her, he asked no better lot, and a hope that she might give him the right to do this began to be strengthened as he saw that he was the one person to whom she turned. When she felt that support was needed, she clung to Reuben for it. When the time came that she thirsted for consolation, it was at his hand she sought it. She listened to his counsel and acted on his advice, trusting everything to his guidance, until—the elasticity natural to youth gradually asserting itself—she began to feebly struggle back to the every-day life of the present and the feverish hopes for the future.

Mrs. Pascal had been dead nearly six months now, and though the abiding loss of her mother was as fresh and green to Eve as when she first saw her, yet, during the weeks which had elapsed since her visit to Reuben May, she had regained a considerable portion of her health and her energy.

Her visit to Polperro was now a settled fact, and Reuben had agreed to house her furniture until she came back to claim it.

This past time, with its interchange of letters, its suspense, its anxieties, had been one of great excitement to Eve, and surely its outpour of sweets and bitters, at one time set suddenly flowing, at another as suddenly checked, had well-nigh distracted Reuben May.

But now all was settled, every arrangement made, and nothing more remained to be done but to sit idly down and wait for the hour of departure.

The order of her journey, and the means by which it might be accomplished, had been left entirely to her uncle, and a couple of days since a sailor-looking man had come to say that the *Mary Jane* of Fowey was now unlading at Oates' Wharf, and her captain had bid him run up and say, that he'd been asked by Zebedee Pascal at Polperro to convoy round a niece of his that he'd find in London ready and waiting to go with him, that the captain's name was Triggs, and if all went well the *Mary Jane* would get under weigh on Sunday morning about four o'clock, so that miss had best come aboard the night before. Eve, having already received notice that Captain Triggs of the *Mary Jane* was to be her escort, accepted the invitation, and was now waiting for Reuben's arrival to accompany her down to the wharf.

Those who have made a first solitary venture out into the world will perhaps know the contending emotions which were stirring within Eve. Later on, when life seems one long journey, with few or many resting-places, the whole matter is altered, and we know that nothing will be nearly as good or as bad as we anticipate; our expectations grow more moderate and are not so easily damped; our regret is less keen, but more lasting. Eve's feelings had reached the stage when all else is merged in the great longing to be gone, and the dread of going. Naturally affected by external surroundings, the sight of the furniture disarranged, huddled together, and swathed for protection in bits of carpet and such like wrappings, filled her with melancholy; a melancholy which seemed shared in by the cat, who sat miserable and disconsolate on the tied-up bed, giving pantomimic mews which had no sound, but much sadness. The window was curtainless, the fireplace untidy and choked with torn-up paper and useless rubbish; the sea-chest, turned for the occasion into a table, was littered with the remnants of that last meal which Reuben had impressed upon her it was necessary she should fortify herself with; the rush candle standing on the mantelshelf near, just gave enough light to deepen the shadows and darken the corners into fit lurking-places for imaginary terrors.

Eve's courage seemed to die within her; her heart grew troubled and reproachful. Could she be doing wrong? Ought she to have stayed working at her lace-mending, as her mother had wished her to do? Did it not seem as if she was forsaking that mother in thus going away from all, that while they were together had grown familiar? True it was that she could no longer see her, hear her speak, listen to her words; but she could go to the grave where she was laid, and in sweet commune there feel such a depth of rest and peace as never came at any other time. For oft beside that daisied mound a spirit seemed to stand, and there, 'twas not the breeze that stirred the air, but the soft rustle of angelic wings. When she was gone, would that dear presence hovering come, and watch, and watch in vain, for her who had left it lonely and alone? The thought pierced Eve like an arrow, and, overcome by quick remorse, she flung herself down and wept so passionately that, though Reuben, who had just mounted the stairs, knocked sharply before entering, she neither stirred nor spoke. He opened the door: it needed but the sight of her bowed figure beside the old chair, with her face hidden down in the seat where her mother had always sat, to tell him what was giving rise to the struggle through which Eve was passing. The vision of past days when he was sure to find the two in loving company, the dear motherly face, the cheerful tidy room, all came crowding before him, and contrasted bitterly with the present grief and discomfort. A mist swam before Reuben's eyes, and he made an involuntary pause. Unknown to himself, the next few moments would decide one of those turning-points which, few or many, come to all our lives, and his hand held the balance; his next action, nay, almost his next word, would fix the future. How will he act? what will he say?

Alas, poor Reuben! had he loved less

he would have ventured more, but great love is seldom venturesome; held back by a thousand emotions, it stands trembling on the threshold over which a more selfish passion strides triumphant. Untutored in love's ways, ignorant of the arts by which it is ensnared, Reuben was guided by a compassion so tender, that his heart let its own anguish and its great yearning be swallowed up in the one desire to spare his beloved pain and keep her from suffering. Gulping down the torrent which sprang to his lips, he sounded the knell to his fate by saying, in a forced tone of commonplace surprise:

'Come, come, Eve; why, what are you thinking of? I thought to find you ready and waiting for me; it won't do, you know, to drive things off to the last minute, or if so——' and the rest of the sentence was drowned by the noise he made in unnecessarily dragging a box from one side of the room to the other, after which, expending a further surplus of energy in giving vigorous pulls to sundry stray pieces of rope, Reuben turned to find Eve standing up ready and waiting.

At sight of her wan face all his firmness seemed to desert him, and involuntarily stretching out his hand he laid it on her shoulder.

'Eve,' he said, 'my dear one, if you could see my heart torn in two to see you suffer!'

But the sympathy had come too late, the recoil had been given; those first few words had turned the depth of feeling back upon herself, and the heart which lay cold and dull within Eve no longer felt reproach for herself, nor craved sympathy for her suffering.

'I'm quite ready now,' she said, with a little movement which told Reuben more effectually than words that his small show of affection was displeasing to her. 'I've said good-bye to everybody, I'll take these small things down, and tell the man to come, and you'll help him with the boxes on to the truck?'

'Then ain't you coming up again?'

'No; I shall go slowly on, and you can overtake me;' and, without another look at him, or at the room she was leaving, Eve went downstairs and passed out of the house into the street.

Oh! for how many a weary night and day was that walk to dwell in Reuben's memory; the starless sky, the silent gloom of the all-but deserted streets seemed to shadow forth the unknown future, while every onward step but widened the barrier which had insensibly sprung up between him and Eve, who moved along mechanically with her face impassible, and her manner so distant and cold, that the last fond words which lay crowded on Reuben's lips were chilled before he found courage to speak them.

But if anything is to be said it must be said at once, for the bridge has been crossed, the last turning made, and the dark, silent river is near, bearing on its waters a small forest of masts, one of which belongs to the little barque which is to carry Eve away.

Away! the thought flashed before Reuben as if he only now, for the first time, realised that they were going to part; all the pain, fear, dejection that lay scattered over the last two months seemed to crowd itself into the anguish of this present moment, a great shadow of foreboding rose up to encompass him, a cloud of desolation spread its gloom around him, and, nerved by the keenness of this agony, he seized Eve by the sleeve.

' 'Tisn't too late !' he gasped; ' Eve, for the love of God don't go to this place ! No, I can't tell you what it is,' he added, in answer to the frightened look of amazement with which she stopped to regard him ; ' but something's come over me all of a sudden that, if we part now, we part for ever ; the words seem set ringing in my ears, and pull at my heart-strings like a passing bell. There's still time to turn back ; it needs only a word from you, Eve !' he pleaded.

But Eve's eyes were turned from his, gazing away far beyond him.

Did the balance of destiny again tremble? if so, it was only for an instant; for before Reuben had time to urge more, her face quivered, her whole frame relaxed, and, with a voice full of sadness, she sighed out despondingly:

'Tis too late now, Reuben—too late, too late!'

And the words had scarce left her lips when some one from behind touched Reuben on the shoulder, and a man came forward, who said:

'If I'm not signalising the wrong party by mistake, my name is Triggs, and forrard lies the *Mary Jane*.'

And after this, save for the commonplace 'Good-bye' of friends, there was no further leave-taking; but when the morning dawned, and by its light the little vessel slowly stole away, a woman's eyes were vainly strained towards the shore, striving to pierce the mist which hung around, and hid from view a man who, waiting, stood until the creeping day lifted the veil and showed him a blank of water.

Then Reuben knew the little ship had gone, and as his heart sank down it seemed to bid farewell to Eve for ever.

## CHAPTER IV.

THE little barque which was carrying Eve away from her home and its early associations was bound for Fowey, between which place and London Captain Triggs traded.

On her way to Fowey, some few miles further up the coast, the *Mary Jane* would have to pass Polperro, but as it would not be possible for her to lay to, or land her passenger, it had been agreed that Eve was to go on to Fowey, at which place her uncle would probably be found waiting to receive her.

Many an hour had Eve passed in pleasant anticipations of her coming journey, and how it was to be made, indulging her imagination by picturing the three or four days of perfect idleness, when there would be nothing to do but sit and watch the rolling sea, and feel the ship ride gaily o'er the dancing waves.

Alas, poor Eve! a very different experience was hers to tell, when, towards the close of the fourth day, she emerged from the tiny cabin, out of which, since the time they had lost sight of land, she had never stirred, and feebly struggled upon deck to find they were already inside Fowey harbour, and nearing the quay at which she supposed they intended to land.

The day had been wet and stormy, and the mists hung heavy and thick over the crooked, winding streets of Fowey, and the wooded heights of its opposite shore.

At any other time Eve would have been struck with the new beauty of the scene around her; but now, weary in body and sick at heart, all her thought was, had her uncle come, and how much further was there to go? Would this shouting and bawling to 'cast off' and 'hold on' never cease? The babel of strange sounds which naturally accompanies most nautical efforts seemed to daze Eve's untutored senses, and she had just begun to relinquish all hope of this state of confusion ever coming to an end, when the welcome voice of Captain Triggs sounded in her ears, saying:

'I half fancy your uncle ha'n't come, or he'd be aboard afore now, I reckon.'

'Perhaps he does not know that the vessel has got here yet,' said Eve, 'and if not, whatever shall I do?' she added anxiously, the last remnant of endurance vanquished by the fear of spending another night on board.

'Well, he'd calkilate on our being here some time to-day, though I 'spects he'd reckon on us gettin' in a brave bit earlier than us has, by which raison us may find un stuck fast at the King o' Proossia's; howsomedever, you'm all right now, for my house is only over to Polruan there, and my missis 'ull make 'ee comfortable for the night, and you can go on in the morning, you knaw.'

'Thank you,' said Eve, faintly, 'but I should like to make sure first that uncle has not come.'

'Iss, iss; all right, us'll rin up to Mrs. Webber's to wance; I can go with 'ee now, so come 'longs,' and he held out his hand to help her down from the cask upon which, in order to get out of the way, she had seated herself. 'Steer clear o' they ropes,' he said, as they crossed the deck, after which poor Eve, abandoning herself to the certainty of a watery plunge, came with a flop down into one of the several small boats which lay bobbing about near enough to form an unsteady sort of bridge across to land.

'There us is, you'm right 'nuf now!' exclaimed Triggs cheerily, as Eve paused for an instant at the top of the few steps to take breath. 'I'll warrant you won't be in no hurry to volunteer for the next voyage,' he added, laughing, as he caught sight of her pale face. 'Why, you be a poor hand on the watter surely, I don't believe that you've so much as held your head up for five minutes since us started.'

'I feel just as if I was on board the ship now,' said Eve, trying to steady her staggering footsteps. 'I do hope that I shall find my uncle here, I am longing to be at my journey's end.'

'Well, I hardly know what to say till I've bin inside, but I half fancy if he'd come, us should ha' sin un about somewheres afore this,' and he turned to take another scrutinising look around before entering the inn, in front of which they now stood.

It was an odd, queer-looking place, even in those days reckoned out of date and old-fashioned. Irregular stone pillars raised it some twelve feet from the ground making it necessary, in order to gain the door, that you should mount a perilously steep flight of steps, up which, with an alacrity familiarity alone could have rendered safe, Captain Triggs ran, giving an unnecessary duck of his head as he passed under the swinging signboard on which was depicted the once universally popular Prussian hero.

A minute or so elapsed, and then he emerged again, this time bidding Eve to 'come on,' as it was 'all right,' in accordance with which invitation she followed his direction, and stepped from across the threshold into a room which by contrast looked so bright and cheerful that, with a sigh which seemed to relieve her burdened spirit of half its weight, she sank down into the nearest empty chair.

'Why, who have 'ee got there then, Capen Triggs?' demanded a voice which proceeded from a railed-off portion of the farther end of the room; ''tis never she that Sammy Tucker's bin axin' about—he spoke as if her was a little maid. Why, do 'ee go near to the fire, my dear, you looks all creemed with the cold and as wisht as can be.'

'Here, take a drop o' that,' said one of the men, pushing a glass of steaming grog towards her, while the others moved up on the settle so as to leave the nearest seat to the fire vacant. 'Don't be afeard of it, 'tis as good a drop o' sperrits as ever was paid toll for—eh, Mrs. Webber?' and he gave a significant wink towards the buxom landlady, whose jolly rubicund face, and stout though not ungainly figure, was quite in keeping with its background of ornamental kegs, glasses, and bottles, filled with cordials and liquors seldom seen except in houses frequented by wealthy and well-to-do people.

The fear of giving offence made Eve raise the glass to her lips, but the smell, forcibly reminding her of the remedies which had been pressed upon her during her recent voyage, so overcame her that she was obliged to hastily set it down with a faintly-spoken apology that she wasn't feeling very well, as she had only just come off the sea.

'Have 'ee come with Capen Triggs, then? not all the way, for sure?'

'Yes, I've come all the way from London.'

'Have 'ee though! and where be goin' to—who's your folks here, eh?'

'I'm going to Polperro,' replied Eve,

somewhat amazed at her interlocutor's outspoken curiosity. 'I have an uncle living there.'

'Her's own niece to Zebedee Pascal,' broke in the landlady, who, having by this time learnt from Captain Triggs all he knew of Eve's history, was unwilling that the first batch of news should be given out by any other than herself; 'her mother's a died and her's left all alones, and Zebedee's wrote to her to come down to Polperro, and bide with they so long as ever her likes, or for good and all if her's so minded to. He'd ha' come for her hisself, but they ain't a landed yet; so he's sent word in by Sammy Tucker that her's to go back with he. 'Twas never thought they'd be so late in, so Sammy was all ready to start by four o'clock; though now, when 'tis nigh 'pon the stroke o' six, he ain't to be found no place.'

'Why, I knaws where he's to,' said one of the audience. 'I seed un, as I come up along, sittin' into my cousin Joe's;' and, moved by the look of weary anxiety on Eve's face, he added, 'Why, if 'ee likes, I'll run and see if he's there now, shall I? and tell un to look spry too, for 'tain't every day he's got the chance o' car'yin such a good-lookin' young woman up behind un.'

The compliment, half-sheepishly spoken, brought the colour into Eve's pale face, and it deepened as the eyes of each one present were turned in her direction.

''Tis a purty-faced maid, surely,' was buzzed about the room, until the landlady, out of pity for Eve's confusion, gave a dexterous twist to the conversation by saying,

'I can't father her on any o' the Pascal folks, though, they're all such a dark-featured lot; 'ceptin' 'tis Adam, and he's as fair as he's franty.'

A general nod had just given consent to the truth of these remarks, when the man who had volunteered to fetch Eve's escort arrived, accompanied by him and Captain Triggs, who had run down to take another look at how things were going on on board the *Mary Jane,* and lend a hand in bringing up Eve's box.

'Well, here you be at last, then,' exclaimed Mrs. Webber, with a nod of remonstrance at Sammy Tucker's unexplained absence; ''tis a hunderd to one her hasn't gone to Polruan afore this—slippin' off and nobody able to tell where you're to. I wouldn't ha' bin in your shoes, I can tell 'ee, if you'd a had to shaw your face to Joan Hocken and nothin' better than empty sacks behind 'ee.'

A general laugh was caused by this sally, followed by a few more home-thrusts at Sam Tucker's expense, which made him not sorry to seem engrossed in the ceremony of an introduction, which Captain Triggs briefly effected by giving him a lurch in Eve's direction, as he said:

'There lies yer cargo, Sammy; and my advice is, get it aboard and up stick and away so quick as you're able.'

'Hope I see 'ee well, miss,' said Sam, trying to recover his equilibrium, after falling against two men whose heads he had brought rather sharply together.

'I say, young chap, where might you be a steering to, eh?' exclaimed one; while the other, with a very decided anathema, hoped that he might have no more of that sort of game, or he'd know the reason why—words spoken in a tone which made Eve move with greater alacrity than she had before thought possible, and, nodding a shy farewell to those around her, she hastily moved from her seat out to the space in front of the bar, where another five minutes had to be spent in declining the various cordials which Mrs. Webber was bent upon fortifying her with. Then the horse had to be brought round, the boxes carried to a place of safety until some boat was found to convey them to Polperro, and finally Captain Triggs put in his head and announced all ready for starting.

'But I'm never to go like that?' exclaimed Eve, aghast at seeing nothing but the small horse on which Sam Tucker was already mounted. 'Oh, I can't! Why, I should be certain to fall off; I was never upon a horse in my life!'

'No reason why you shouldn't begin now, my dear,' laughed the landlady, who had accompanied Eve to the door. 'Why, what be feared of? Bless the maid, 'tis only to hold tight on by Sammy, and you'll be right enuf!'

'But my box! how's that to go? Oh, I thought surely they'd have sent a cart!'

'A cart?' echoed a voice from among the party, all of whom had come from within to witness Eve's departure. 'I say, Sammy, how many carts has thee got to Polperro, eh?'

'Why, wan,' answered Sammy, stolidly.

'And when you wants he, you puts un

in a boat and pulls un round, doan't 'ee ?'

This observation seemed to afford much merriment, which Mr. Tucker not relishing, he called out:

'Come, miss! us must be thinkin' about goin', you know.'

'Iss, that you must,' said Captain Triggs, decisively. 'Now put your foot there, and I'll give 'ee a hoist up,' and, suiting the action to the words, he all but sent Eve over the other side.

This little lurch, as the captain called it, was, however, soon remedied; and before Eve had time to enter another protest, the horse, weary of standing, put an end to the matter by setting off with a very tolerable amount of speed, and away they went clattering along the narrow length of North Street, Eve far too frightened to be able to think of anything beyond how best she might keep tight hold of her companion.

At length, to her momentary relief, they stopped, but only for a moment; for Sammy, discovering that the ferryboat was on the point of starting, gave vent to some vigorous halloos, which he kept up, until by dint of 'Gee up's,' 'Come hither, then,' and 'Woa's,' they at last found themselves safely standing in the capacious ferry-boat.

'Be 'ee goin' to get down?' asked the ferryman.

But before Eve could answer, his companion bawled out:

'Noa, noa! let be where her is; the watter's comin' in so fast we'm knee-deep here already.'

'Her's gotten a leak in her some place,'

said the first man, by way of apology for his mate's impetuosity. 'I can't think where 'tis to though, and us haven't time to lay her up by daylight to see neither; but I reckon us had better do so 'fore long, or 'er'll carry us all to bottom. Her's drawing watter now most powerful strong.'

'Wa-al, you wunt get no toll from we, 'less you car's us safe,' piped a chorus of women's voices from the stern, where they sat huddled together, trying to keep their feet out of the water which flowed in with every length the boat took. 'The young woman up there's got the best of it, I think.'

'And so her seemeth to think, too,' said the outermost of the party, ' to look how her's houldin' on to un. Why, do 'ee think you'm goin' to lost un in crossin', my dear?' she said, addressing Eve, who heard her words, although she heeded not, for life must be secured, though it were by holding on with might and main to Sammy Tucker's back.

So the women laughed, and Sammy simpered, but Eve neither spoke nor relaxed her hold until they were out of the boat, up the steep hill, and fairly jogging quietly along what seemed, by comparison, a level road.

Then Eve ventured to turn her eyes from her companion's dusty coat, and cast them timidly around. Even in the open country the light had by this time begun to fade away, so that between the high narrow hedges, along which their road lay, it was grey and shadowy. Mile after mile was passed, with nothing more to be seen than walls of tangled briars and brushwood, whose out-stretched trails Eve had constantly to shrink back from.

Sometimes a gate or opening would disclose the undulating country beyond, the white mists hanging thick and low over the slopes of turnips or stubble. Fortunately for her, her companion was not given to loquacity, so that, except when by a wave of his short stick he signified that this farm was Poljan, and that Withers, or that the dark object rising on the right was Lansallos Church, 'Where they all lies buried to,' he preserved a merciful silence, thus affording Eve the full liberty of inwardly groaning at the misery she endured, by being jolted over the rough stones with which the old pack-horse road was promiscuously strewn.

'It seems a very long way,' she said

at last, as, after reaching the foot of a particularly steep descent, they seemed about to enter a valley shut in by what, to Eve, looked like mountains. 'Is that the sea?' she added eagerly, as a sound of water fell upon the ear.

'The say!' repeated Sammy; 'Lor' bless 'ee, there ain't no say here; that's the watter,' he explained, raising his voice, for the stream seemed, for a minute, to be running a race with them. 'Up back there,' and his unexpected turn nearly sent Eve into the road, 'the mill is. That's where I lives to, with Joan's mother; her married my feyther—only feyther's dead now, so th' mill's mine. Uncle Zebedee's wife was Joan's mother's sister, so that's why her lives with un; and as you'm his niece, too, they axed me to bring 'ee home. They didn't think ye'd bin so late in, d'ee see? or I reckon they'd ha' sent word for 'ee to bide the night at Mrs. Webber's.'

Interested in this explanation of her new family ties, and the relation they bore to one another, Eve was about to inquire if she should see Joan, and what she was like, when Sammy, catching sight of the distant lights, was fired by the laudable ambition of making a good entry into the village which they were now fast approaching; and giving a vigorous application of his stick, away went the horse past a row of houses, through the open hatch-doors of which, Eve caught glimpses of domestic interiors and social groups, evidently disturbed by the hores's clatter, for at the sound they jumped up, peered out into the darkness, and flung after them an inquiring ' Good-night?'

'Iss, good-night; 'tis only me!' roared Sammy, an answer which was apparently satisfactory, as the next 'good-nights' sounded more hearty and cheerful.

Then a sudden narrowing of the road, and they were in the street—had turned a corner—forded a stream—and, oh, welcome finale! had come to their journey's end; and before Sammy could apply the knob of his stick, the house-door had opened, a stream of light from within was sent out into the street, discovering a girl, who, after a moment's hesitation, ran to the horse's side, tip-toed up to seize hold of Eve's hands, exclaiming, in a pleasant voice, as she did so:

'Why, is this Eve? I'm Joan Hocken, so we'm kind o' cousins, you know! Why, whatever have they bin doin' with 'ee till this time o' night? I was looking for 'ee hours agone. There, wait till us gets a stool, my dear, and then you'll be able to step down easy.'

Eve tried to return this greeting with as much cordiality as she could command, but no great strain was put upon her, for Joan asked a dozen questions, without waiting for half of them to be answered, and by the time Eve had managed to extricate herself and her garments, had stepped down and stretched her cramped limbs, Joan was in full possession of all that had taken place during the state of expectancy which had preceded her arrival.

'Take care o' the step,' said Joan, pushing open the hatch-door for Eve to enter, while she lingered behind to aim a few parting arrows at Sam Tucker, in whom Joan's presence seemed to have aroused the power of continued laughter.

The opportunity thus afforded, Eve spent in casting a look round the room, a moderately-sized one, but unusually narrow for its length. A cheerful fire burnt on the hearth, and the light of its fierce bright blaze played on the walls, one side of which was taken up by an elaborately-furnished dresser, while in an opposite corner stood a capacious glass cupboard. The rest of the furniture was of a fashion far above anything Eve had expected to see, so that, without being able to bestow much separate notice on the things individually, the effect produced was a sudden thought that her uncle must be much better off than she had imagined him to be; this made her wonder where he was, and Joan coming in at the moment, she said:

'Isn't Uncle Zebedee at home? Shan't I see him to-night?'

'No, the boats is away, and us don't 'spect no news of 'em 'til to-morrow or next day, so us two 'll have to put up with wan 'nother's company 'til then, and ofttimes after, if you bides here, which I hope,' she added, smiling, ' you will, when you comes to knaw us a bit better.'

Eve looked up to show that she appreciated this kindly speech, and their eyes meeting, they let them linger for an instant, while each made a shy inspection of the other's personal appearance.

Joan was a bright-faced, good-looking girl, with quick dark eyes and a white skin which no exposure seemed able to tan; she was rather below the middle height, and had a round compact figure which was set off to advantage by her quilted petticoat and handsome coloured chintz gown, the style and pattern of which had immediately caught Eve's notice ; the handkerchief, too, which was tucked into her bodice was many degrees finer than anything Eve possessed; and to crown all, the cap which she wore was actually trimmed with real French lace. In the surprise caused by the sight of such an unexpected display, Eve entirely forgot what Joan's face was like, while Joan, who generally took in the complete costume of any one before her, had not even noticed that Eve's dress was plain after a fashion very unusual in those parts. Her eyes were still resting admiringly on the face before her, struck by its being quite unlike any she had ever seen ; the delicately-cut features, the fair yet not white skin, the deep-set eyes with their drooping fringe of black lashes, all had a separate charm for Joan.

'Don't 'ee never have no colour?' she said, putting the question which arose to her mind.

'Colour!'

''Iss, in yer cheeks, I mean.'

'Oh no!' and Eve put up both her hands as if trying to remedy the defect. 'I don't know how it is,' she said, 'that I'm so pale and sallow-looking.'

'Saller! do 'ee call it?' laughed Joan; 'I wishes I was saller, then. I b'lieve if I was to drink whole tubs o' vinegar—and I have drunk quarts,' she nodded emphatically—'I should still have a colour like a piney. But there, you may get your health better away from the town; and if so, you won't want to go back never no more, will 'ee?'

The coaxing tone of voice said so much

more than the words, that Eve, unused to the sweet singing cadence of a West-country voice, felt grateful to the girl for her kindly feeling.

'If they're all like you, I'm sure I shall like to stay as long as you want me to,' she said, with a little quaver; 'but there's uncle to know yet. I'm such a stranger to you all,' she sighed, 'that I don't know anything about anybody, who they are, nor nothing.'

'Oh, that's soon made straight!' exclaimed Joan, well pleased at any opportunity that allowed her tongue to run. 'You sit down there now,' and she pulled forward a large stuffed elbow-chair, 'and have your tay and that comfortable, and I'll tell 'ee all about our folks. First there's Uncle Zebedee—well, there's only one o' his sort goin', so 'twould be waste o' time to tell up about he. He'll be better to 'ee than twenty fathers, though Adam's got no cause to say that. Adam's his son, us two maidens 's cousin.'

'Who's Adam?' asked Eve, more for the sake of showing a polite attention than out of any particular interest she felt in the conversation, for the sense of ease produced by the comfortable seat and refreshing tea was beginning to take effect; a lazy indifference to anything that did not necessitate exertion was stealing over her, and though she repeated, 'Oh, my cousin is he?' it came upon her as a fact of no importance, and just after that there came a blank for a moment, and then the room here suddenly changed to the one she had left behind, and it was no longer Joan but Reuben May sitting opposite to her; a jerk of her nodding head, and this transformation was upset; and Eve opened her eyes with a sudden stare which made Joan burst into a laugh, as she jumped up, saying :

'Why, I declare you've bin to sleep, and no wonder too, poor sawl, after the time you've had of it. Come 'longs, and let's be off to bed, and I'll tell 'ee the rest tomorrow.'

'Don't think that I was asleep,' said Eve, making an effort to rouse herself; 'I only shut my eyes for a minute, but I heard all you were saying.'

Joan laughed doubtingly.

'I did indeed,' urged Eve. ''Twas something about Adam—he's my cousin, isn't he?'

''Iss, that's all right,' laughed Joan; then, stooping to pick up Eve's cloak and hood, she looked in her face for a moment, gave a little pinch to her cheek, and said, as she did so, 'and I wonder whatever he'll think of his new-found relation?'

## CHAPTER V.

HE next morning Eve awoke to find that much of her fatigue was gone, and in its place a languid depression was left, often the sequence to an undue amount of exertion. She got up and dressed herself, but the feeling still had possession of her; so that, when on going downstairs the woman, who did the rough work of the house, told her that Joan had just stepped out for a few minutes—'Her said her'd be back in half an hour to most—' Eve, with the hope that the air might freshen her, decided that she too would go for a little stroll. Finding herself outside the house, she stood for a few moments debating which would be the best way to go—up or down? or across over the narrow bridge under which the brook, swollen by recent rain, was impetuously flowing? It could not matter much, and, influenced by the novelty of walking across the water, she retraced the street by which on the previous night she had made her entry into the village. Here it struck her that it would be a pity to go over exactly the same ground again, so at the corner she turned her steps up the hill, until some yards farther on, the road becoming again divided, she took the left-hand path, and found herself all at once in the midst of a labyrinth of houses, some of which went up steps, some went down; some were tolerably large, others barely more than huts. But however the external part of their dwellings might differ, the inhabitants seemed actuated by one spirit, which led them to leave off doing whatever they might be about, run to the door, and openly stare at the stranger. 'Comed last night,' 'Sammy Tucker,' 'Zebedee Pascal's own niece,' were whispers which came floating past Eve as she hurried on, rather put out of countenance by finding herself the object of such general observation. At another time she would have been far less affected, but now her spirits were low and uneven, and it was an unspeakable relief to her to find herself past the houses and between a long low shed which formed part of a building-yard, and a heap of piled-up, roughly-hewn blocks of stone, over which some children were running, too engrossed in their play to pay any heed to Eve.

'How foolish of me to take notice of such things,' she said to herself, reprovingly; and then the feeling of loneliness came over her again with redoubled strength. She would not admit to herself that she was regretting that she had left her home, and, with a determination to give no place to such a doubt, she tried to busy herself by thinking if the room would be all right and her furniture safe, and Reuben kind to the cat, which, though an animal he abominated, he had promised to take care of for her sake.

For her sake! Yes, Reuben would do most things that she asked him; he was indeed a dear, kind friend to her, and she almost wondered what she could want altered in him. He loved her, did all he could to please her, only asked for her to care for him in return; and did she not do that? A tenderness, such as she had never felt before, stole into Eve's heart. It was as if the yearnings which from afar Reuben was sending after her were being answered; an instant more and an echo would carry back to him the open-sesame to her love, of whose birth that soft fluttering sigh seemed the herald.

Surely nobody was watching her! Eve looked up with the coy bashfulness of a maiden who fears she has betrayed her secret, and at the sight which met her eyes a cry of sudden surprise escaped her, for there lay the sea, the vast, dashing, wave-ridden sea, which must be spreading out away far beyond that hill which, overhanging, hid it from her sight. A moment's pause, and then at full speed, with a pent-up impatience, which made her avert her eyes so that she might look no more until she had reached the top, and could command the whole, Eve ran forward, never stopping until, the height reached, she stood with an awed face, and, slowly turning, gazed upon the scene spread out before her.

To right, to left, around, above, below, the sea and sky mirrored each other, both vast and fathomless and blue, save where they mingled, and together framed themselves within a belt of silvery light.

A tremor ran through the girl's slight frame, her whole body quivered with emotion; the glory of that longed-for sight mastered her, its grandeur overpowered her, and, clasping her hands, she flung herself down against the slope and let her tears come unrestrained until, her sobs abating, her heart seemed eased, and she was able to look around her with returning calmness.

From the point on which she stood not a habitation was to be seen; the cliffs, which, grass-crowned and green, were kissed by the clouds above, ran broken and bare down to the sea below, their grey base lapped and washed by the foaming waves; the wind, soft but cool, told tales of having lingered by the gorse and played among the thyme, a fresh scent from which came up in sweet reproach, trodden under by the footsteps, Eve was at length unwillingly obliged to turn towards the house.

With many a lingering look behind, slowly she came along until, some half-way down the steep descent, the little village opened into view.

Many a year has passed away since Eve Pascal stood arrested by the beauty of that scene. Towns have dwindled into hamlets, villages have been turned into cities; in not a few places the very face of the earth is so changed that men would stand strangers on the spot where they lived and died, but not so here; a street added to, a road made, a few houses more or less, and Polperro now is as Polperro then—quaint, picturesque, and hidden from the world around. Clustered on the ledges of the rock 'the village coucheth between two steep hills,' forming the entrance to a narrow, winding valley, shut in by high slopes with craggy summits. As a foreground spreads out the sea, its force held back on one side by the hill descending headlong into its water, and on the other by the peak whose pinnacles stand towering black and bare.

All this is still the Polperro of to-day, but the people are changed into a quiet, simple fishing folk, with nothing but a dim memory—fast fading out—of those men and women of a bygone day who made and broke laws according to the code they themselves had instituted; were bound together by their given word which none had ever broken; punished a thief, and scorned a lie, with hearts as honest and consciences as clear as if they had never heard of a free-trader, and were ignorant of what was meant by a 'good run of goods.'

Sheltered from observation, with a safe and commodious harbour, most difficult of approach save to the amphibious population who had been reared amid its rocks, Polperro seemed marked out as a stronghold for the life of daring deeds and hairbreadth escapes in which the hardy, reckless sailors of that time revelled.

The rage for excitement then manifested in London and the great towns by a pervading spirit of gambling, highway-robbery, and betting, had spread itself into the country under cover of poaching, and reached the coasts in the shape of smuggling; and how could a pursuit be dishonest or disgraceful in which, if all did not bear the risks, none refused the benefits?

The rector and the magistrate drank the brandy, their wives and daughters wore the lace, and gossiped over the tea; even the excise officer shouldered the tub laid at his door, and straightway became blind to all that was going on around him. tI could hardly need more than this to satisfy minds untutored and consciences not burdened by scruples, that, though their trade might be unlawful, the offence was venial; and so universally had this spirit worked and spread in Polperro, that at the time when Eve came among them, by whatever trade they might call themselves, a common interest bound the whole community together: the farmer, the miller, the smith, the shopkeeper, each had his venture; the serving man or maid brought his or her hoard, the child its little nest-egg, trusting it to the keeping of those who were sure to turn the slender store to fortunate account.

The aged and infirm watched the sign of a land of goods with eager interest, for the workhouse and parish relief was unknown, and those past labour supported themselves by the sale of articles brought to them free of freight.

If Eve's father had ever entered into any details of this life, from which a press-gang had taken him, and to which his early death had prevented him returning, Mrs. Pascal had never thought fit to repeat them to her daughter; and when Eve left London it was with the conviction that she was going to her uncle, a fisherman, whose means she expected to find slender, and his abode as humble as the one she was leaving behind her.

Weakened by fatigue as on the previous night her powers of observation were, she could not help being struck by the visible marks of superiority in the furniture, and a plenty amounting to extravagance on the table. Then Joan's dress and lace cap only increased the bewilderment, so that, though politeness checked its utterance, her mind was full of curiosity, which she felt she had no right to satisfy by taking advantage of Joan's evident weakness for giving information.

Until the previous evening when the two girls met, Eve had known nothing about Joan, except that her uncle's letter had said that she wouldn't be alone in the house, as his late wife's niece lived there and looked after things for him. For some reason the idea which Eve had formed in her mind about this niece was that she must be a sober, sedate, middle-aged person; and it was no small relief to her to find that she had been completely mistaken, and had for a companion the bright, merry-faced girl who now, as she reached a before unperceived bridge, darted towards her, exclaiming :

'Well, for certain I thought you'd run home agen, or was pisky-laid or something. Why, wherever had 'ee got to? When I went away I left 'ee sleeping as fast as a top.'

'Is it late? have I been long?' asked Eve. 'Oh! I am sorry; I didn't think I'd stayed hardly a minute after I'd got to the top, but it is so lovely—oh! I could spend my day looking at it.'

'Looking at it!' repeated Joan; 'looking at what? Where have 'ee been to the top to? Why, the maid's mazed,' she laughed; 'there's nothin' up there to look at.'

'Nothing to look at!' exclaimed Eve, reproachfully, 'and the beautiful lovely sea all around you?'

'Well, but if there is, there's nothin' 'pon it. Awh, my dear, if you'm so fond of looking out and watching the say, wait a bit 'til the boats is comin' in, that's the time; and I'll tell 'ee what we'll do this afternoon, if so be you'm so minded—us'll go up top o' Hard Head, and if us catches sight of 'em comin' in, we'll run down so fast as can and tell the news, and you shall have *kimbly* for telling it. Why, don't 'ee know what kimbly is, then?' she said, seeing by Eve's face that she did not understand her. ''Tis the present you gets for being the first to bring word that the boats be in sight, then they knaws 'tis all right,' and she nodded her head significantly; 'some o' the women are such poor sawls, always fainty-hearted, and thinking their men's certain to be took.'

'Took where?' asked Eve, innocently.

But instead of answering her, Joan only said laughingly:

'Oh! away, any place, back o' beyond or somewheres near it; but come 'longs home, do, or 'twill be dinner-time afore breakfast's over.'

At breakfast the bountiful supply which appeared again raised Eve's surprise, and she could not refrain from saying, in a voice which betrayed her wonderment:

'Are we going to have tea again?'

'Yes,' said Joan. 'Why, don't you like it?'

'Oh! I like it, only it's so dear.'

'Not in this place,' interrupted Joan; 'if we minded to we might be drinking tay all day long, ah! and not only tay, but rum and brandy, as much as you like to call for. It's only to ask and to have, and cut and come again, in uncle's house.'

'I didn't think to find things any way like that,' said Eve, 'I thought,' she added, hesitatingly, 'that uncle would be more the same as most working folks are, not over well-to-do.'

'Oh, isn't he though!' returned Joan, with an evident pride of relationship. 'Why, besides his two boats, he's got a farm and land, and houses too, and this house stuffed from top to bottom with everything you can tell up about. Silver plate, Indji china, and glass, and I don't know what all; nice pickings for Adam's wife, whenever he chooses to take one!' she added, with satisfaction at the visible surprise her communication was producing.

'Adam isn't married, then?' said Eve.

'No, there's a chance for *you*;' and Joan gave a little laugh, followed by a gravetoned 'and a very good one too, if th' other men look at 'ee with my eyes.

Adam's one that over-valleys everything he hasn't got, and never cares a button for what's his'n; but there, he's spoilt, ye know, by all the maidens here runnin' after un, and ready to go down on their bended knees if he but so much as holds up his finger to 'em. I'd never let no man say that o' me,' she said, the quick colour mantling into her face. 'I'd die for his love 'fore I'd be kept alive by his pity; that's what my mother calls my masterful sperrit, though,' she said, trying to divert Eve's attention from thinking that her declaration was influenced by any personal feeling.

'Yes, till last night I didn't know you'd got a mother,' said Eve. 'Uncle Zebedee wrote in his letter that a niece kept house for him, so I thought perhaps you were like I am,' and she glanced down at her black dress.

'Well, I don't know that I'm much better off. Father was Uncle Zebedee's chum, and mother was Aunt Joanna's sister, so when father died, and mother married again, Aunt Joanna took me, and somehow I don't seem as if I belonged to mother; and I'm very glad I don't, neither, for I couldn't abide to be pitched among such a Methodie lot as she's married into.'

'My mother was very drawn towards the Methodists,' said Eve gravely; 'she didn't live to be a member of them, but she dearly loved going to their chapel.'

'Well, I don't mind the chapel-going, cos' o' the hymn-singin' and that; it passes the time Sundays, 'specially come winter, when, 'ceptin' 'tis for a weddin' or a funeral, t' seems ridiklous to toil all the way up to church. But there, I'm done with the Methodies now; I shan't never have no opinion o' they agen.'

'And for why?' asked Eve.

'Well, I'll tell 'ee for why: what right has wan o' their praichers from Gwennap pit, a man as had never set foot in Polperro before, to spy out uncle and fix upon un to make a reg'lar set at, tellin' up 'bout the smugglers and all Mr. Wesley had wrote agen 'em. Mr. Wesley may be all very well, but he isn't everybody; and if so be he says what they puts down to un, why, all I can say is, 'twas better he was mindin' his own business.'

'But what need uncle take offence for?' said Eve; then, with a quick resolve to set her doubts at rest, she added: 'I can't see what it had to do with him. Uncle hasn't got anything to do with the smuggling, has he?'

'Well, that's best known to uncle hisself,' said Joan, rising from the table. 'Only mind this, Eve: whenever you hear people talking anything against what they don't know nothin' about, you just tell 'em that you've got a uncle and cousin as never did a thing they was ashamed of in their lives. And to be set 'pon like that, in a chapel, too, where you'm foced to sit still with yer mouth shut; 'twas no wonder that uncle swored he'd never set foot inside no such place agen—though 'tis very hard 'pon me, after havin' got un to go there—and now, Sundays, 'tis drink, drink, as bad as iver.'

Eve's heart sank within her; a thousand undefined fears took possession of her mind, casting their shadows on her troubled face, which Joan, quick to note, tried to clear away by saying:

'Awh! you know what men be when a passel of 'em gets together, and there's nothin' more to do but tellin' up th' old stories over and over again; then, every time they can't think of nothin' else, 'tis empty their glasses. And uncle's one who's all very well so long as he's had nothin', or he's had enough; but betwixt and between you might walk with yer head in yer hand, and then 'twouldn't be right. Jerrem's th' only wan that can manage un at they times and sich.'

'Jerrem!' repeated Eve, 'who's he—another cousin?'

'Well, yes and no; everybody belongs to Jerrem, and he belongs to nobody.'

'Why, how can that be?' laughed Eve.

'Why, 'cos he can't claim blood with none o' us here, nor, so far as he knows, with none no place else. He was washed ashore one Christmas Eve in th' arms of a poor nigger-black, who never fetched the shore alive. 'Twas more than twenty year agone, on a terrible night o' weather; the coast for miles was strewed with wrecks. I can't tell 'ee how many ships was washed ashore in Whitsand Bay, and all about up to there. To one of 'em the poor black man must ha' belonged, and tried to save his life and the child's too; though he couldn't ha' bin his own neither, for Jerrem's skin's as clear as yours or mine. He was naught but a baby like, I've heerd 'em say, and couldn't spake a word. Oh! but Aunt Joanna she did love him dearly, though; 'twas she gived un the name o' Christmas, through it being Christmas Day when ole Uncle Jeremy, what used to live to the Point, runned in and dropped un in her lap. "There, missis," he says, "I've a broffed 'ee a Christmas box." So they took and called un Jeremiah Christmas, and that's his name to this very day; and he don't awn to no other, only we calls un Jerrem for short. Poor aunt, I've a heerd her tell scores o' times o' the turn she got when she saw 'twas a baby that th' ole chap had dropped.'

'Had they got any children of their own, then?'

'Awh, yes! Adam was a good big boy, able to talk and rin about; and the little toad had got a jealous heart inside un then, for the minnit he seed aunt kissin' and huggin' the baby, he sets up a screech, and was for flying at un like a tiger-cat; and to aunt's dyin' day he could never abide seein' her make much o' Jerrem.'

'That wasn't showing a very nice disposition, though,' said Eve.

'Well, no, no more it was; still I've often wished aunt would do other than she did, and not be so tooked up with Jerrem's coaxin' ways as she was, for, with all his kissin' and cossetin' of her, when her was lain low, poor sawl, 'twas easy to see which heart had been most full of love for her. But there, we'm all as we was made, ye know, some to show and some to feel.'

## CHAPTER VI.

ALTHOUGH the two girls spent most of the afternoon on Hard Head and the heights around, nothing was to be seen of the expected vessels, a disappointment which, Joan seeming to feel, Eve tried to get up some small show of having a share in, although in reality it was a relief to her that nobody was coming to intrude upon, perhaps to dispel, her present state of happiness—a happiness so complete that she felt as if she had been suddenly transported into the land of her dreams and fancies, only that this reality exceeded the imagination in a tenfold degree.

In the beginning, at each turn she would seize Joan by the arm, and excitedly make a fresh demand upon her sympathy, until, finding that Joan only laughed at such enthusiasm about a scene which familiarity had robbed of its beauty, Eve relieved herself by giving vent to long-drawn sighs of satisfied content. With something of that rapture akin to which the caged bird hails its newly-gained freedom, did this town-bred maiden gaze upon the unbroken space before her.

Whichever side she turned, her eyes fell on a scene, every feature of which was new to her. Landward, the valley with its sloping craggy sides. Seaward, the broad blue belt of waters, out into which the distant headlands stretched with the shadowy dimness of an unknown land. Overhead, the sun shone hot and bright, so that Joan, languid and drowsy, threw herself down and gave way to her inclination to doze; while Eve, well pleased to have her quiet, sat silent and rapt in the beauty around her.

Not a sound came to break the stillness, save when the gulls went soaring overhead with croaking cries, or the bees grew noisy over the nodding thistles. Surely in such a place as this sin and sorrow must be unknown, for, with those one loved on earth, who could be sorrowful here? This thought was still in her mind, when Joan, suddenly awakened, proposed they should descend; and, after stopping to cast a last look from the Chapel Rock, they took their way back to the village.

'Oh my, what steps!' exclaimed Eve, as she prepared to follow Joan down a worn-away flight, roughly cut out of the solid rock.

'Fine place for pattens, my dear,' laughed Joan, as, having recklessly reached the bottom, she stood waiting, inwardly tickled at Eve's cautious descent.

The sound of voices had by this time brought to the door of a cottage, situated at the top of the landing-place, an old woman, who, after giving a short-sighted scrutiny to Joan, said:

'Awh, it be you, be it? I couldn't think w'atever giglet 'twas comin'. How be 'ee, then?'

'Oh, all right,' said Joan. 'Are you pretty well?'

'Iss, there ain't much amiss wi' me. I's iver so much better than I war thirty year agone. I doan't wear no bunnet now, nor no handkecher, nor that; and I can see without no spectacles. Awh, bless 'ee, if 'twasn't for my legs I should be brave, but they swells terrible bad; and that's where I'm goin' to, if so be they'll car' me so far, to Tallan beach there, to walk 'em down a bit 'pon the pebbly shore: the doctor says 'tis the thing to do, and the more rubbly the better. Who be you, then?' she said, as Eve landed herself on the flat beside them.

''Tis Uncle Zebedee's niece from London,' answered Joan, with becoming pride in her City connection.

'Awh, whether she be or no! wa-al,

you'm come to the right place here for maidens—men to marry and money to spend. Awh, I wishes I was young agen. I'd tell 'ee 'bout it, and me as could car' me two gallons o' sperrits and a dollup o' tay, besides lace and chaney, and was knawed up to Plymouth and for miles round. Why, I've bin to the clink afore now,' she said triumphantly: 'and they threatened me with Bodmint Gaol wance, but not afore I'd marked my man, bless 'ee: he car'd Poll Potter's score on his body to his grave, I'll warrant 'em he did.'

'Ah, you've bin one o' the right sort, Poll,' said Joan; 'folks now ain't what they used to be in your day.'

'No, tine-a-by, not they,' returned the old woman, contemptuously; ''tis all for stickin' yerself up for fine madams, now;

dressin' out and that. This is the thing—' and she caught hold of the lace on Joan's kerchief—' and ruffle sleeves, forsooth! Shame upon 'ee, Joan, and yer uncle too, for lettin' 'ee wear such fal-de-lals; and Zebedee a sensible man as knows the worth o' such, for over a guinea a yard and more!'

'It hasn't got nothin' to do with Uncle Zebedee,' said Joan, with a toss of her head; ''twas Adam gave 'em to me, there now,' and she passed her hand gently over the delicately textured frill which shaded her somewhat over-coloured elbows.

'A bit o' sweetheartin', was it? But there, don't 'ee trust to 'un Joan, he isn't a-thinkin' of *you*, take my word for that;' and she raised her voice to call after Joan, who, at the first words of warning, had ran down the remaining steps.

'Don't you make too sure o' that!' Joan called back, turning round under pretence of seeing that Eve was coming.

'All right, only doan't you nayther,' said the old woman, emphatically. 'So you be his chield?' she said, looking at Eve as she passed by; 'and a nice rapskallion rogue he war,' she added, with a sigh; 'but for a' that I was mazed after un, though he couldn't abide me—more's the pity, p'r'aps, for he might ha' bin alive now, though that's nothin' much, neither. 'Tis a poor tale of it when 't comes to naught else but lookin' on; if 't warn't for the little they brings me, freight free, and the bit o' haggle I has o'er it, I'd as soon be out of it as here.'

The concluding sentence of these reflections was lost upon Eve, as she had already overtaken Joan, whose flushed face betrayed the annoyance old Poll's words had caused.

'Why, Joan, I do believe you're a sly one,' said Eve, 'and that, for all you say, Adam's more than a cousin to you.'

'No, indeed he's not,' replied Joan, quickly; 'so don't take that into yer head, Eve. You'll soon hear from all around who's got a soft place for me, but 'tisn't Adam, mind; folks brought up together from babies never turn into lovers, somehow.'

'Don't you think so?' said Eve. 'Oh, I don't know that; I've heard tell of several who've thought different, and have married.'

'Have 'ee? What, people you've knowed!' said Joan, earnestly; 'they who've always lived together in one house as we've done! I should like to hear about 'em, if 'twas only out of curiosity's sake.'

But unfortunately, when put to the test, Eve was unable, by further experience, to substantiate her statement, and could only repeat that, though she couldn't bring their histories clearly to her mind, she felt certain she had heard of such people; and Joan shook her head disappointedly, saying, in an incredulous voice :

'Ah, I can't credit it; it doesn't seem likely to me that ever such a thing could come to pass.'

And she turned aside to speak to a comely-looking woman, who came out to the door of a near-by house which they were passing.

'Well, Joan, who've 'ee got there?' she called out.

While Eve, in order to allow of the question being freely answered, turned to look at the quaint weather-beaten pier. Fortunately it was high-water, and the unsightly deposits, often offensive to the nose as well as the eyes, were hidden from view.

Everything seemed bathed in sunlight, and pervaded by a soft drowsy quiet. A group of aged men leaned over and against the bridge, enjoying a chat together; some boys lounged about the neighbouring rocks, and seemingly played at catching fish; with these exceptions the whole village seemed delivered up to women.

''Tain't much of a place to look at now,' said a voice near.

And turning, Eve found it came from

the woman belonging to the house into which Joan had by this time entered.

'Polperro's a proper poor wisht place when the boats is out.'

'Why, are there more boats than are here now?' asked Eve.

'What d'ee mane—than these here? Why, bless the maid, how do 'ee think they'm to reach Guarnsey and places in such like as they? Why, did 'ee never see a lugger? No? well, then, us has got somethin' to show 'ee for all you've come fra London.'

'Oh, you've many things here that I wouldn't change for all the sights London can show,' said Eve, promptly.

'We have? Why, what be they, then?'

'The country and the sea all around, and everything so still and quiet. I was thinking, as I sat looking out upon it all up on top there, that the people here must be forced to be very good!'

'My life!' exclaimed the woman, turning round to Joan, ''tis time her was cut for the simples. Why, do 'ee knaw,' she said, addressing Eve, 'that there ain't a place far nor near that's to—— But there,' she interrupted, 'I won't tell 'ee. I'll only ax 'ee this much—come down here this time next week, and tell me what ye thinks of it then. Still and quiet, and foced to be good!' she repeated. 'Well, I'm blest! why, was 'ee born innicent, or have 'ee bin took so all of a suddent?'

Poor Eve blushed confusedly, feeling, without knowing how, that she had been guilty of displaying some unusual want of sense; while Joan, annoyed at her being so openly laughed at, exclaimed angrily:

'Don't take no notice o' what she says, Eve; she's always telling up a passel o' nonsense. And so 'tis just what Eve says,' she added, sympathetically; 'a stoopid old place half its time, with nobody to see, and nothink to look at. If uncle don't come by to-morrow, we two 'll go to Looe or Fowey, or somewheres; we won't die o' the dismals in this old dungeon of a hawl. Why t' sodgers 'ud be better than nobody, I do declare!'

''Tis so well to wish for t' pressgang, while you'm 'bout it,' laughed the woman; 'and I don't know but you mightn't give 'em a welcome neither, if they'd only find their way up to Crumplehorne and fall in with our Sammy a-twiddlin' his thumbs. Have 'ee took her up to see yer mother yet?' she asked, jerking her finger towards Eve, whose attention was by this time completely engrossed in examining the contents of the well-furnished dresser. 'I say,' she said, answering Joan's pout and shake of the head, 'there'll be a pretty how-de-do if you doan't; her was down here sighing and groanin' her insides out 'cos somebody'd ha' told her they seed 'ee to the wrastlin' match. As I said, "Why, what be 'ee makin' that noise about, then? There was as honest women there as your Joan, or her mother afore her." I han't a got patience with anybody settin' their selves up so, 'cos they chance to come fra Bodmint. "Fower wa-alls and a turnkey," as old Bungey said, when they axed what he'd seed there; and that's purty much about it, I reckon, leastwise with most that makes that journey. Still, if I was you, Joan, I'd take her up, 'cos her knaws her's here; Sammy's a-told her that.'

Joan spent a few minutes in reflection, then she said:

'Eve, what d'ye say? wilt 'ee go up and see mother?'

'Eh, Joan! mother—what, your mother? Yes, I should like to very much. I was so taken up with all this beautiful china,' she said, apologetically, 'that I wasn't listening to what you were talking about.'

'Doesn't her clip her words?' said the hostess, who was a relation to Joan on the father's side. ''Tis a purty way o' talkin' though, and's all of a piece with her. You've a lost somebody, my dear, haven't 'ee?' she asked, looking at Eve's black gown.

'Yes, my mother,' said Eve, surprised at the tone of sympathy the questioner was able to throw into her voice.

'Ah, that's a sore loss, that is. I've a

lost my awn mother, so I can tell. Poor old sawl! I thinks I see her now! When we childern had bin off, nobody knows how long, and her worritin' and thinkin' us was to bottom o' say, her'd come out with a girt big stick and her'd *leather* us till her couldn't stand, and call us all the raskil rogues her could lay her tongue to. I often thinks of it now, and it brings back her words to me. "You may find another husband," her'd say, "or have another chield, but there's niver but the wan mother." And some o' that chaney there was hers. Well, that very cup and sarcer you'm lookin' at now belonged to she! and so you take it, my dear, and keep it. No! nonsense, but you *shall*, now!' for Eve was protesting against accepting such a present. ''Twill only get broked up into sherds here; and if her was alive, you'd a bin welcome to th' whole dresserful, her was such a free-handed woman! Chaney, tay, liquor, no matter what—so long as she'd got, she'd give.'

'I think you must take after her,' said Eve, rather embarrassed by such unexpected generosity; 'but I really feel as if I was taking advantage of your good-nature. I shall be afraid to admire anything again, though that'll be a hard thing to do in a place like this, where everybody's got such lots of lovely things.'

'Oh, 'twon't be long afore you'll have as good as any one; for, for sure, they'll niver let 'er go back agen. So you'd better write to the baws you've left behind and tell 'em so to wánce.'

Eve gave a shake of her head, which served the double duty of disowning the impeachment of a beau, and bidding farewell; and the two girls turned up the street, and only waiting to deposit Eve's cup in a safe keeping-place, they took their way towards Crumplehorne.

The road recalled to Eve's recollection the way by which she had come, though it seemed impossible that it was only on the previous evening that she had traversed it for the first time. The varied scenes she had looked upon, the sensations she had passed through, had spread the day over a much longer space of time than that occupied by twenty-four hours. Already Joan had made her feel as if she was a friend whom she had known for years. Even the people whom she casually met broke the ice of first acquaintanceship by such a decided plunge,

10—2

that she was at once at home with them. Altogether a new phase of life had opened for her, and had suddenly swallowed up her anxieties about the present, and her regret about the future.

During the whole day, since the early morning, not one thought of Reuben had entered her mind; a test, had she been given to analyse her feelings, of her perfect contentment. For as long as Eve was happy, Reuben would be forgotten; let disappointment or regret set in, and her thoughts veered round to him.

'Why, you've turned silent all to once,' said Joan, tired of her own five minutes' reflections.

'I was thinking,' said Eve.

'What about?' asked Joan.

'Why, I was thinking that I couldn't believe 'twas no more than last night I passed by here—oh! with such a heavy heart, Joan!' and at the remembrance her eyes swam with tears.

'And for why?' said Joan, in some surprise.

'Oh, because I began to feel that I was coming to where you'd all be strange to me; and I wondered whether I'd done right in leaving my own home where mother and me had lived together so long.'

'Hadn't 'ee any else to leave behind but the thoughts o' your mother?' interrupted Joan, practically.

'No.' Then, feeling this was not quite true, she added: 'That is, nobody that I minded much—not that I cared to leave. I had somebody that didn't like me going, and begged me to stay—but that was only a friend.'

'A friend?' repeated Joan, incredulously—'a friend that sticketh closer than a brother, I reckon. Come now, you may so well tell me all about it; I'm sure to get at it sooner or later. What's his name, eh?'

'Oh, I don't mind tellin' you his name,' laughed Eve. 'Reuben May, that's his name; but 'tisn't he I want to speak of—'tis you, Joan, for makin' me feel so at home all at once. I shall never forget it, never!'

And as she turned her face toward Joan, the drops which had trembled in her eyes fell on her cheeks.

'Why, what nonsense next!' exclaimed Joan, impulsively threading her arm through Eve's, and hugging it close up to her; 'as if anybody could help being kind to 'ee. 'Tis only to look in your face, and you can't do no other; and mind, 'tis none o' my doin's that you'm here,' she continued, following out her own train of thought. 'I was that set agenst your comin', as you never did. I couldn't abide the thoughts of it. Adam, and me too, took on with uncle ever so, when he would have 'ee come; but 'twas no use, there was no turnin' un; and now I wouldn't have it otherwise for iver so. You'm so altogether differnt to what I looked for; I thought you'd be mimpin' and mincin', and that nothin' 'ud please 'ee, and you'd be cuttin' up a Dido with everything and everybody; 'stead o' which 'tis as if I'd know'd 'ee all my life, and you'd bin away and come back agen.'

'Oh, I am so glad,' said Eve, laughing in the midst of her tears; 'for when you've lost everybody, as I have, something in your heart seem always pining after people's love.'

'Which you mostly gets, I reckon,' said Joan, smiling. ''Tis that innicent sort o' look you'm got, and yer mild way o' speakin', that does it, I 'spects. But you must pluck up a spirit afore the men'— for Eve had been telling her how entirely unaccustomed she was to any but female companionship—' and be ready with an answer afore they speak, so impident as some of 'em be. They know 'tis no use tryin' it on with me, though. I gives 'em so good as they brings, any day; and that's what men like, you know—plenty o' courage, and a woman that isn't afraid o' anything or anybody; for, no matter how I feel, I'd die afore I'd show any fear.'

'But I should show the fear, and die too,' said Eve.

'Not a bit of it,' laughed Joan; 'I'll give 'ee a lesson or two so that you shan't know yourself for the same.' Then, suddenly stopping and drawing down her face, she said: 'But "there's a time for everything," said Solomon the wise, and that time ain't now, for there's the mill, and 'tis in here that my mother lives. And Eve,' she continued, turning round in the act of giving the gate a hoist preparatory to swinging it open, 'if so be mother should begin about uncle and they, don't you take no heed, 'cos what she says doesn't lie deeper down than her tongue, and she only says it to keep in with the chapel-folks.'

Eve was spared the awkwardness of any reply, by having to bestow all her attention on picking her steps through the mud by which the gate was surrounded, for from most of the people carrying their corn to be ground, and not unfrequently waiting about until the process was accomplished, the approach to the mill was seldom or never anything but a slough, of a consistency varying with the state of the weather. A few yards on, this miry path turned off to the right, leaving a tolerably free space of well-washed pebbles, in the midst of which was the dwelling-house, the door of which was conveniently placed so that it commanded a full view of the out-gate. In a straight line with this door, the upper half of which, after the prevailing fashion, was left open, a little round table was set, and behind this table Eve, drawing nearer, perceived an elderly person, whom she supposed must be Mrs. Tucker. But, notstanding that by this time the two girls were close by, Mrs. Tucker's face continued immovable, her eyes fixed, and her fingers knitting away as if no mundane object could possibly engross such steadfast attention.

The gaze so completely ignored the presence of her visitors, that by the time Joan had got up to the door, Eve had found ample time to take a critical survey of Mrs. Tucker's personal appearance, which formed such a contrast to Joan's, that it was difficult to reconcile it with the close relationship which existed between them.

Mrs. Tucker seemed tall, flat, and bony; her dress was drab, her kerchief black, and her cap, under which her hair was all hidden, was fashioned after the model of a Quaker's. Still her face, though stern, was not unpleasing, and its form and features were, on the whole, better modelled and more delicately cast than her daughter's.

'Well, Joan!' she said at length, with a touch of displeasure in her voice.

'Well, mother!' answered Joan, with a corresponding modicum of defiance.

Then there was a pause, during which Joan evidently waited for her mother to say something to Eve, but this hope being vain, she was forced into saying, with a trifle more aggression :

'Ain't you goin' to say nothin' to Eve, mother? I brought her up a-purpose, fancyin' you'd like to see her, p'r'aps, and 'ud be put out if I didn't.'

And stepping on one side, she threw Eve into the foreground, and obliged her to advance with the timid air of one who is uncertain of her welcome.

'I don't know why I should be expected to know people afore I've heerd their names,' said Mrs. Tucker, stiffly; 'but, if this is Eve — why — how do you find yourself?' and she made just sufficient pause between the two parts of her sentence to give the idea that the greeting, prompted by politeness, had been curtailed by principle.

'I feel better to-day,' said Eve, growing confused under the scrutiny she was undergoing.

'My son-in-law, Samuel, told me that you seemed very tired by your journey.'

'Yes,' answered Eve, feeling her indifferent treatment of Samuel might be the cause of this cool greeting; 'I fear he thought me but poor company. I hardly spoke a word all the way.'

'Well, if you'd nothin' to say, 'tis so well to hold yer tongue; as I tell Joan, 'tis but a poor clapper that's allays on the tinkle. Why didn't you come up to dinner then, Joan?' she said, turning to her daughter. 'We mightn't have got dainties to set Eve down to, but we've allays got somethin' to eat, thank the Lord.'

'I couldn't tell but what uncle might be home, and we can't stay now long, for they may be in any hour.'

'Ah, then uncle hasn't seen Eve yet? I should say he'd be disappointed not to find her more featured like her father's family.'

'I don't know why he should be, then,' said Joan, sharply. 'I can't tell who she's featured after, but somebody a sight better-looking than any o' the Pascal lot.'

'That's as people see,' said Mrs. Tucker, grimly.

'Oh yes,' returned Joan, recklessly; ''tis free thought, and free speech, and free trade here, and long life to it, I says.'

'And what do you say, Eve?' asked Mrs. Tucker.

'Eve can't say anythin' about what she don't know nothin', can ye, Eve?' said Joan; 'but as far as she's sin, she likes the place dearly, and the people too, and she don't intend to go back to London never no more.'

'Oh, Joan, Joan! don't say that!' exclaimed Eve, trying to give a more pleasant turn to the discord which was evidently impending between the mother and daughter.

While Mrs. Tucker said:

''Tis early days to make up your mind,

seeing you haven't sin yer uncle yet, nor he you. Joan allays forgets that there's more than she has got a voice in matters.'

'No, Joan don't, mother; and you'll see that there'll be more than uncle and me beggin' her to stay. Adam hasn't seed her yet,' and the girl looked up with an expression of defiance.

'That's true,' replied Mrs. Tucker, without altering a tone or a feature; 'Eve has got to see both the baws—Adam and Jerrem, too. 'Tis to be hoped you'll take to Jerrem, Eve,' she said, glancing in Joan's direction, 'or your uncle will be sore put out; he seems to have got his heart set 'pon you and Jerrem makin' a match of it.'

'He hasn't done nothin' o' the sort,' returned Joan, fiercely; 'and 'tisn't right in you to say so, mother, 'cos uncle, in a joke-like, said somethin' in a laughing way, but he didn't mean it no more for Jerrem than he did for Adam; and, as Eve hasn't sin neither of 'em, 'tis as likely she takes to one as t'other, and more when she knows 'twould be disappointin' me, for I loves Jerrem dearly, Eve, and I don't care who knows it, neither.'

'I think if I was a young pusson, I should wait 'til I was axed afore I was so very free in offering my company to anybody,' said Mrs. Tucker, worked at last into some show of anger.

'Oh, no need for that,' laughed the irrepressible Joan. 'So long as we understands each other, whether Jerrem tells me or I tells he, it comes to the same thing; and, now that we've had our haggle out, mother, I think 'tis so well us goes;' and she jumped up, but so heedlessly that the tucked-up train of her gown caught in the handle of a neighbouring cupboard-door, and she had to stand still while Eve endeavoured to disentangle it.

'There's one thing I'm glad to see,' said Mrs. Tucker, taking note of the two girls as they stood side by side, 'and that is, that Eve's clothes is consistent, and I hope she's got the sense to keep 'em so, and not be a-bedizenin' herself out with all manner o' things as you do, Joan. I'm fairly fo'ced to close my eyes for the dazzle o' that chintz. Whatever you can be thinkin' o' yerself to go dressin' up in that rory-tory stuff, I don't know. Does it never enter yer poor vain head that yer miserable body will be ate up by worms some day?'

'They won't eat it up any the more 'cos o' this chintz gown, mother. Ain't it sweet and purty?' she added, turning to Eve. ''Tis a rale booty, that 'tis; there isn't the like of it in the place. 'Twas gived to me a Christmas present,' she added significantly, while the displeasure deepened in Mrs. Tucker's face, so that Eve tried to throw a little reproof into the look she gave Joan, for she saw plainly enough that mother and daughter were at cross-purposes about somebody, and Joan was bent upon teasing.

Whether Joan noticed the expression, she could not tell; but, after a minute's pause, she broke out passionately, saying:

'How can 'ee find it in yer heart to act as ye do, mother, never havin' a good word or a kind thought for a poor sawl who hasn't nobody to cling to natural-like? Any one 'ud think the religion you'm allays preachin' up would teach 'ee better than that.'

'Everybody in their place, that's my motter,' said Mrs. Tucker, whose stolid manner was vividly contrasted with her daughter's excitable temperament; 'and the place o' strangers ain't that o' childern. Now, 'tis of no use bidin' here to cavil, Joan,' she continued, seeing that Joan was about to answer her. 'I've used the same words to your aunt, and your uncle too, scores o' times, and said then, as I say now, that a day may come when they rues it; and all I pray for is that my misgivins' mayn't come to pass.'

'Iss; well, I think you may let that prayer bide now, mother!' exclaimed Joan; 'there's plenty else things to pray for besides that, and people too. There's me; you've always got me on hand, you know.'

'I don't forget you, Joan; you may make your mind easy o' that,' said Mrs. Tucker.

'Well, here's Eve, you can give her a turn now.'

'Very like I might do worse, for I dare swear Eve ain't beyond needing guidance more than other young maidens.'

'No, indeed,' said Eve; 'none of us are too good, and I often have the wish to be different from what I am.'

'Ah, 'tain't much good if you don't go no further than wishin',' said Mrs. Tucker; 'so far as wishin' goes, you might sit there and wish you was home, but you wouldn't be a step the further near to it.'

'That's true,' broke in Joan, 'for I've bin wishin' myself home this hour and more, and so I should think had Eve, too.'

'Oh, I dare say,' said Mrs. Tucker. 'I know very well that I'm no great company for young folks; but a time may come—when I'm dead and gone and mouldin' in my grave, though you may both be left behind—to prove that the words I've a spoke is true; for we all do fade as a leaf, and are born to sorrow as the sparks flies upwards;' and with this salient remark, Mrs. Tucker allowed the two girls to depart, Joan fairly running, in her anxiety to be out of the place, the further gate of which she flung open with such force that it closed behind them with a swinging noise that seemed to afford her much relief, and she gave vent to a loud sigh, saying:

'Now, Eve, isn't mother too much for anybody? She just works me up till I could say anything. There, don't 'ee look like that at me, 'cos 'tis her fault so much as mine. She knows what I am, and what sets me up, and yet that's the very thing she pitches on to talk about.'

'I fancy you say things, though, that vex her too,' said Eve, smiling.

But Joan did not return the smile; her face grew more cloudy as she said:

'Perhaps I do—I dare say; but you don't know all the ins and outs. Some day, happen, I may tell 'ee—'t all depends.' And she gave another sigh. 'But 'tis shameful to set Adam up agen Jerrem, and that mother's sure to do if ever she finds the chance. She'd tell another story if she'd got to live with 'em both, and was allays tryin' to set all straight between the two, as I am; and Jerrem so madcap and feather-brained as he is, and Adam like a bit o' touch-paper for temper.'

'I half think I shall like Jerrem better

than I shall Adam,' said Eve, with a sly look, intended to rouse Joan from her grave mood.

'Do 'ee?' said Joan, with a smile which began to chase away the cloud from her face. 'But no; you haven't seen the two of 'em together yet, Eve. When you do, I'll wager 'tis Adam you'll choose.'

Eve shook her head.

'I'm never one to be taken by looks,' she said. 'Besides, if he was everybody's choice, why isn't he yours—eh, Mrs. Joan?'

Joan feigned to laugh, but in the midst of the laugh she burst out crying, sobbing hysterically as she said:

'Oh, because I'm nothin' but Cousin Joan, to be made much of when there's nobody else, and forgot all about if another's by!'

Eve stood amazed. This sudden shifting mood was a mystery to her; she hardly knew what to say or do. Surely her speech could not have pained Joan? if so, how? and why? She was still hesitating, and thinking what comfort she could offer, when Joan raised her head with the visible intention of saying something—but in a moment her attention was arrested; she took two or three steps forward, then, apparently forgetful of all else, she exclaimed:

'It must be they! Yes, there's another! Quick, Eve! run, 'tis the boats! One o' 'em's in sight, and most like 'tis uncle's! If we don't look sharp they'll be in 'fore we can get home.'

## CHAPTER VII.

JOAN in front, Eve within speaking-distance behind, the two girls made all haste to reach the village, where Joan's anticipations were confirmed by the various people with whom, in passing, she exchanged a few words.

Coming within sight of the house, a sudden thought made her turn and say:

'Eve, wouldn't 'ee like to see 'em comin' in, eh? There's light enough left if us looks sharp about it.'

Eve's lack of breath obliged her to signify her ready assent by several nods, which Joan rightly interpreting, off she ran in advance to leave a few necessary directions about supper; after which she joined Eve, and together they hurried on towards a small flat space just under the Chapel rock, where a group of people were already assembled.

The sun was sinking, and its departing glory hung like a cloud of fire in the west, and flecked the sea with golden light; the air was still, the water calm, and only rippled where the soft south-west breeze came full upon it.

Several small vessels lay dotted about, but standing out apart from these were two of larger size and different rig, one of which just headed the other.

' 'Tis uncle's in front,' said a weather-beaten old fellow, turning round to Joan, who, for Eve's convenience, had taken her stand on the rising hillock behind. 'T' hindermost one's the *Stamp and Go*.'

'Never fear, the *Lottery* 'll niver be t' hindermost one,' said Joan, boastfully.

'Not if Adam's to helm,' laughed another man near; 'he'd rather steer to 'kingdom come' first, then make good land second.'

'And right he should, and why not?' exclaimed Joan; 't' hasn't come to Adam's luck yet to learn the toons they play on second fiddles.'

'Noa, that's true,' replied the man, 'and 'tis to be hoped 't never will; t' ud come rayther hard 'pon un up this time o' day, I reckon.'

'I 'spose uncle's had word the coast's all clear,' said Joan, anxiously.

'Awh, he knows what he's about. Never fear uncle; he can count ten, he can. He wouldn't be rinnin' in, in broad day, too, without he could tell how the coast's lyin'.'

'Why don't they sail straight in?' asked Eve, following with great interest each movement made.

''Cos if they hugged the land too tight they'd lose the breeze,' said Joan. 'Her don't know nothin' 'bout vessels,' she said, apologising for Eve's ignorance. 'Her's only just comed here; her lives up to London.'

'Awh, London, is it!' was echoed round, while the old man who had first spoken, wishing to place himself on a friendly footing with the new arrival, said:

'Awh, if 'tis London, I've a bin to London too, I have.'

'What, living there?' asked Eve

'Wa-al, that's as you may choose to call it: t'warn't much of a life, though, shovellin' up mud in the Thames river fra' mornin' to night. Howsomdever, that's what they sot me to do, "for chatin' the King's revenoos,"' he quoted, with a comical air of bewilderment. 'Chatin'!' he repeated, with a snort of contempt, 'that's a voine word to fling at a chap vur tryin' to git a honest livin'; but there, they'm fo'ced to say sommat, I 'spose, though *you* mayn't spake, mind. Lord no! you mun stand by like Mumphazard, and get hanged for sayin' nothin' at all.'

'Joan, look! why, they've got past!' exclaimed Eve, as the foremost of the two vessels, taking instant advantage of a puff of wind, gave a spurt and shot past the mouth of the little harbour. 'Isn't it in here they've got to come?'

'All right; only you wait,' laughed Joan, 'and see how he'll bring her round. There, didn't I tell 'ee so!' she exclaimed triumphantly. 'Where's the *Stamp and Go* now, then?' she called out, keeping her eyes fixed on the two vessels, one of which had fallen short by a point, and so had got under lee of the peak, where she remained with her square brown sail flapping helplessly, while the other made her way towards the head of the outer pier. 'Now 'tis time for us to be off, Eve. Come along, or they'll be home before us.'

And, joining the straggling group who were already descending, the two girls took their way back to the house, Joan laughing and vaunting the seamanship of her cousin, while Eve lagged silently behind with sinking spirits, as the prospect of meeting her new relations rose vividly before her. Putting together the things she had heard and seen, the hints dropped by Joan, and the fashion in which the house was conducted, Eve had most unwillingly come to the conclusion that her uncle gained his living by illicit trading, and was, indeed, nothing less than a smuggler — a being Eve only knew by name, and by some image which that name conjured up. A smuggler, pirate, bandit—all three answered to an ancient, black-framed picture hanging up at home, in which a petticoated figure, with a dark, beringleted face, stood flourishing a pistol in one hand and a cutlass in the other, while in the sash round his waist he displayed every other impossible kind of weapon. Surely her uncle could be in no way like that, for such men were always brutal, bloodthirsty; and she, so unused to men at all, what would become of her? among a lawless crew, perhaps, whose drunken orgies might end in quarrels, violence, murder——

'Ah!' and the terrified scream she gave sent Joan flying back from the few yards in advance to see Eve shrinking timidly away from a young fellow who had run up behind and thrown his arm round her waist.

'Why, for all the world, 'tis Adam!' exclaimed Joan, receiving a smacking kiss from the offender, who was laughing heartily at the fright he had occasioned. 'Why, Eve, what a turn you give me, to be sure! Here, Adam, this is cousin Eve. Come here and shake hands with un, Eve. Where's uncle? is he ashore yet? We've bin watchin' of 'ee comin' in. Why, Eve, you'm all of a trimble! Only do 'ee feel her hand; she's shakin' all over like a leaf.'

''Twill pass in a minute,' said Eve, vexed that she had betrayed her nervousness; 'I was thinking, that was the reason.'

'I'm sure I never meant to frighten you,' said Adam, who, now that the group of bystanders had moved on, began offering an apology; 'I took her for one o' the maidens here, or I shouldn't ha' made so free.'

'Oh, you'll forgive him, won't ye, Eve?'

'I hope so,' said Adam; ''twon't do to begin our acquaintance with a quarrel, will it? And I haven't told ye that we're glad to see ye, or anything yet,' he added, seeing that Joan had hastened on, leaving them together, 'though there's not much need for sayin' what I hope you know already. When did you come, then, Cousin Eve, eh?'

'Yesterday.'

'Oh! you didn't get in before yesterday? and you came in the *Mary Jane* with Isaac Triggs?'

'Yes.'

Eve had not sufficiently recovered herself to give more than a direct answer, and as she still felt dreadfully annoyed at her silly behaviour, she had not raised her eyes, and so could not see the interest with which her companion was regarding her; in fact, she was hardly attending to what he said, so anxious was she to find the exact words in which to frame the apology she, in her turn, was bent on making. There was no further time for deliberation, for already Adam had pushed open the door, and then, as he turned, Eve got out:

'You mustn't think I'm very silly, cousin, because I seem so to-night; but I ain't accustomed——' and she hesitated.

'To have a young man's arm around your waist?' he said slyly.

'That wasn't what I was going to say; though, as far as that goes, nobody ever did that to me before.'

'Is that true?' he laughed. Then he called out, 'Here, Joan, bring a candle. Cousin Eve and I want to see each other; we don't know what we're like to look at yet.'

'In a minute,' answered Joan, appearing in less than that time with a candle in her hand; 'there, if you'm in a hurry, I'll be candlestick,' and she put herself between the two, holding the light above her head. 'Now, how d'ye find yourselves, good people, eh? so good-looking, or better than you thought?'

'Ah! that's not for you to know, Mrs. Pert,' laughed Adam; 'but stay, we've got to kiss the candlestick, haven't we?'

'That's as you please,' said Joan, holding up her face to Eve, who was bending down to fulfil the request when Adam caught hold of her, saying:

'Come, come, 'tis my turn first; it's hard if a cousin can't have a kiss.'

But Eve had drawn herself back with a resolute movement, as she said:

'I don't like being kissed by men; 'tisn't what I've been used to.'

'Well, but he's your cousin,' put in Joan; 'a cousin ain't like another man;

though there's no great harm in anybody, so far as I see.'

But Adam turned away, saying:

'Let be, Joan; I'm not one to force myself where I'm not wanted.'

Fortunately, before any awkwardness could arise from this slight misunderstanding, a diversion was caused by the entrance of Uncle Zebedee, whose genial, good-tempered face beamed as he took in the comfortable room and family group.

'Well, Joan,' he said, as Joan ran forward to meet him, 'and who's this? not poor Andrew's little maid, to be sure! Why, I'm glad to give 'ee welcome, my dear. How be 'ee? when did 'ee come? Has her bin good to 'ee, eh? gived 'ee plenty to ate and drink. I'll into her if she ha'n't, the wench!' and he pulled Joan lovingly towards him, holding back Eve with the other hand so that he might take a critical survey of her. 'I say, Joan, what do 'ee say? 'tis a purty bit o' goods, ain't it?'

Joan nodded assent.

'Why, who's her like, eh? not her poor father—no, but somebody I've know'd. Why, I'll tell 'ee—my sister Avice that was drownded saving another maid's life, that's who 'tis. Well, now I never! to think o' Andrew's maid bein' like she! Well, she was a reglar pictur, she war, and so good as she war handsome.'

'That shows us both comes o' one family,' said Joan, rubbing her rosy cheek against the old man's weather-stained visage.

'Not a bit of it,' he laughed; 'but I'll tell 'ee what, she's got a touch of our Adam here, so well as bein' both named together, too. My feyther, poor ole chap, he couldn't abide his name hisself noways, but us two lads, Andrew and me, us allays swor'd that our childern, whether boys or maids, 'cordin' as they com'd fust, should be Adams and Eves, and us kept our words, the both of us, ye see. Here, Adam! he called, ' come hither, lad, and stand up beside thy cousin. I want to take measure of 'ee together, side by side.'

But Adam, though he must have heard, neither answered nor came in; and after waiting for a few minutes, his father, by way of apology, premised to Eve that he had gone up to 'titivate a bit;' while, jerking his finger over his shoulder, he asked Joan, in a stage aside, 'If the wind had shifted anyways contrary.'

Joan shook her head, answering in a low voice that it would be all right, and she would run out and hasten in the supper; and some ten minutes later, while Eve was detailing to her uncle some of the events of her past life—how her mother and she had lived, and how they had managed to support themselves—Adam reappeared, and Uncle Zebedee, pointing to a seat near, endeavoured to include him in the conversation; but whether Eve's past history had no interest for her cousin, or whether he had not quite overlooked her small rebuff, she could not decide. At any rate, he seemed to be much more amused by teasing Joan, and as Joan was by no means unwilling to return his banter while she moved about and in and out the room, the two carried on a very smart fire of rough joking, which gradually began to interest Uncle Zebedee, so that he left off talking to listen; and very soon Eve found herself at liberty to indulge her hitherto restrained curiosity, and take a critical survey of Adam, who lounged on a chest opposite, with his whole attention so apparently engrossed by Joan, as to render it doubtful whether the very existence of such a person as Eve had not entirely escaped his recollection.

Certainly, Adam was a man externally fitted to catch the fancy of most women, and nettled as Eve was by his seeming indifference to herself, she tried in vain to discover some fault of person to which she could take objection; but it was of no use battling with the satisfaction her eyes had in resting on such perfection, heightened by the gratifying knowledge that between them an evident likeness existed. Adam had the same fair skin, which exposure had tanned but could not redden;

his hair, although of a warmer tint, was of a shade similar to her own; his eyes were grey, his brows and lashes dark.

Absorbed in trying to compare each separate feature, Eve seemed lost in the intensity of her gaze, so that when—Adam suddenly looking round—their eyes met (during one of those lapses for which Time has no measurement) Eve sat fascinated and unable to withdraw her gaze. A kindred feeling had apparently overcome Adam too, for—the spell broken—he jumped up and, with something between a shake and a shiver, walked abruptly to the far end of the room.

'Here, Adam,' called out Joan, who had stepped into the outer kitchen, 'don't 'ee go out now, like a dear. I'm just takin' the things up; supper won't be a minute afore it's in, and if it's put back now 'twill all be samsawed and not worth eatin'.'

And, to strengthen her entreaty, she hastened in and set on the table a substantial, smoking-hot pie.

'Why, wherever now has Eve got to?' she exclaimed, looking round the room. 'I left her sittin' there not a minute agone.'

'Eh? what? who's gone?' exclaimed Uncle Zebedee, roused from a cat's sleep in which, with a sailor-like adaptation of opportunity, he was always able to occupy any spare five minutes.

'I think she ran upstairs,' said Adam; 'here, I'll call her,' he added, intercepting Joan as she moved towards the door, which, from the innermost portion of the room, led to the upper part of the house. 'Cousin Eve!' he called out, 'Cousin

Eve! supper's waitin', but we can't begin till you come down.'

'Iss, and bear a hand like a good maid,' chimed in Uncle Zebedee, 'for we haven't had nothin' to spake of to clane our teeth 'pon this last forty-eight hours or so; and I for one am pretty sharp set, I can tell 'ee.'

This appeal being irresistible, Eve hastened down, to find Adam standing so that, when she put her hand on the door handle, he, under the pretence of opening it to a wider convenience, put his hand over hers, leaving Eve in doubt whether the unnecessary pressure was the result of accident or an attempt at reconciliation. One thing was evident, Adam was bent on thoroughly doing the honours of the table; he made a point of assisting Eve himself; he consulted her preference, and offered the various things to her, attentions which Eve, as a stranger and a guest, thought herself, from the son of the house, perfectly entitled to, but which Joan viewed with amazement, not liking, as it was Adam, to interfere, but feeling confident that Eve must be very embarrassed by a politeness not at all current in Polperro, where the fashion was for the men to eat and drink, and the women to sit by and attend upon them.

But Adam was often opposed to general usage, and any deviation was leniently accepted by his friends as the result of his having been schooled at Jersey—a circumstance that Joan considered he was now bent upon showing off, and noting that, do or say what he might, Eve would not raise her eyes, she pitied her confusion, and good-naturedly tried to come to her rescue by endeavouring to start some conversation.

'Did 'ee try to reason with Jerrem, Adam?' she asked, reverting to a portion of their previous talk.

'Reason!' he answered pettishly, 'what good is there in anybody reasoning with him?'

'Awh, but he'll always listen to a soft word,' said Joan, pleadingly; 'you can lead Jerrem anyways by kindness.'

'Pity you weren't there, then, to manage him,' said Adam, in not the most pleasant tone of voice.

'Well, I wish you had bin there, Joan,' said Uncle Zebedee, decisively, 'for I ain't half well plased at the boy bein' left behind; he'll be gettin' into some mischief that 'twon't be so aisy to free un from. I'd rayther be half have spoke to un sharp mysel', he heays minds anythin' I says to un, he does.'

"'Tis a pity then you've held your tongue so long,' said Adam, whose face began to betray signs of rising displeasure. 'I only know this, that over and over again you've said that you wouldn't run the risk of bein' kept waitin' about when he knew the time for startin'. Why, no later than the last run you said that if it happened agen you'd go without him.'

'Iss, iss—'tis true I said so,' said the old man, querulously; 'but he knaw'd I didn't mane it. How should I, when I've bin a youngster mysel', and all of us to Madam Perrot's, dancin' and fiddlin' away like mad? Why, little chap as I be,' he added, looking round at the two girls with becoming pride, ''t 'as taken so many as six t' hold me; and when they've a-gotten me to the boat they've had to thraw me into the watter till I've bin a' but drownded 'fore they could knack a bit o' sense into me. But what of it all? why, I be none the warse for matter o' that, I hopes.'

Adam felt his temper waxing hot within him, and having no wish that any further display of it should be then manifested, he rose up from the table, saying it was time he ran down to the boat again; and old Zebedee, warned by an expressive frown from Joan, swallowed down the remainder of his reminiscences, and kept a discreet silence until the retreating footsteps of his son assured him that he could relieve himself without fear of censure.

''Tis along of his bein' a scholard, I s'pose!' he exclaimed, with the air of one seeking to solve a perplexity, 'but he's that agen anybody bein' the warse o' a drap o' liquor as niver was.'

'Jerrem's one that's too easily led astray,'

said Joan, by way of explaining to Eve the bearings of the case, 'and, once away, he forgets all but what's goin' on around un; and that don't do, ye know, 'cos when he's bin told that they'm to start at a certain time he ought to be there so well as the rest, 'specially as he knaws what Adam is.'

'Iss, and that's the whole rights of it,' returned Zebedee, with a conclusive nod; 'Maister Adam goes spakin' up about last time. "And mind, we ain't agoin' to wait for no wan,"'—and the imitation of his son's voice conveyed the annoyance the words had probably given—'and the boy's blid was got up. 'Tis more than strange that they two, brought up like brothers, can't never steer wan course. I'd rayther than twenty pound that this hadn't happened,' he added, after a pause.

'But how comed 'ee to go when you knawed he wasn't there?' asked Joan.

'I never knawed he warn't there,' replied the old man. 'I can't think how 'twas,' he said, scratching his head in the effort to assist his memory; 'I'd a bin up to Reinolds's, takin' a drap wi' wan or two, and, somehow, I don't mind about nawthin' much more, till us was well past the Spikles; and then, after a time, I axed for the lad, and out it all comes.'

'And what did 'ee say?' said Joan.

'Wa-al, what could I say? nothin' that 'ud fetch un back then. 'Sides, Adam kept flingin' it at me how that I'd a said las' time I wudn't wait agen. But what if I did? I knawed, and he knawed, and Jerrem knawed, 'twas nawthin' more than talk. Moreover which, I made sure he'd ha' come with Zeke Johns in the *Stamp and*

*Go.* But no, they hadn't a laid eyes on un, though they started a good bit after we.'

'He's sure to get on all right, I s'pose?' said Eve, questioningly.

'Awh, he can get on fast enough if he's a minded to. 'Tain't that I'm thinkin' on, 'tis the bad blid a set brewin' 'twixt the two of 'em. If I only knawed how, I'd send un a bit o' my mind in a letter,' he added, looking at Joan.

'Wa-al, who could us get to do it, then? There's Jan Curtis,' she said reflectively, 'only he's to Looe; and there's Sammy Tucker—but Lord! 'twould be all over the place, and no holding mother anyways; she'd be certain to let on to Adam.'

'It mustn't come to Adam's ears,' said Zebedee, decisively. 'Can't 'ee think o' nobody else scholard enuf?'

'If it's nothing but a letter, I can write, Uncle Zebedee,' said Eve rather shyly, and not quite clear whether Joan did or did not possess the like accomplishment.

'Can 'ee though!' exclaimed Uncle Zebedee, facing round to get a better view of this prodigy; while Joan, with a mixture of amazement and admiration, said:

'Not for sure? Well I niver! And you'll do it too, won't 'ee?'

'With all my heart, if uncle will tell me what to say.'

'But mind, not a word before Adam, Eve,' said Joan, hastily; ''cos, if he's minded, he can write a hand like copper-plate.'

'And 'ee thinks two of a trade wouldn't agree, is that it?' laughed Zebedee.

Joan shook her head.

'Never you mind,' she said, 'but only wait till next Valentine's day's a come, and won't us two have a rig with somebody that shall be nameless!'

'Only hark to her!' chuckled old Zebedee, answering Joan's significant look by the most appreciative wink. 'Ah! but her's a good-hearted maid,' he said, addressing Eve; 'and,' he added, with a confidential application of his hand to his mouth, 'if but they as shall be nameless would but voo her through my eyes, her should curl up her hair on her weddin' night in five-pound notes, as her blessed aunt, my poor missis, did afore her, dear sawl.'

## CHAPTER VIII.

S soon as the supper was cleared away, Joan began to set on the table glasses, pipes, and spirits.

'Uncle's sure to bring two or three back with un,' she said; 'and if all's ready there'll be no need for we to hurry back.'

Eve gave a questioning look.

'Why, us is goin' down 'long to see what's up,' said Joan. 'There's sure to be doin's somewheres or 'nother. Besides, you haven't sin none o' the chaps as yet;

and as we don't mean to lose 'ee now us have got 'ee, the sooner that's done the better.'

'Isn't it rather late?' asked Eve, smiling at Joan's insinuations.

'Late! laws no; 'tis only just gone eight, and the moon's risin' as bright as day. Get alongs, like a dear, and fetch down your cloak. Mine's here to hand.'

Eve offered no more opposition. She had no objection to a stroll, and determined in her own mind that she would try and beguile Joan into extending their ramble as far as the cliff-side.

She came downstairs to find Joan already standing in the street chatting to a group of girls who, like herself, were out seeking for amusement.

'Here she is!' said Joan, intimating by

her tone that the former conversation had related to Eve. Whereupon several of Joan's more immediate intimates came forward and shook the new-comer by the hand, while others murmured something polite about 'bein' very glad to make her acquaintance;' and together they all set off in a friendly fashion, exchanging words with everybody they met or passed, and addressing so many of them as uncle this or aunt that, that Eve could not refrain from asking if she was related to any of them.

'Iss, to all of 'em,' laughed one of the girls, Ann Lisbeth Johns by name. 'Why, didn't 'ee know us was all aunts and cousins here? You'd best be careful, I can tell 'ee, for you'm fallen 'mong a reg'lar nest o' kindred.'

'I'm very glad to hear it,' said Eve

politely. 'I hope I may like those I don't know as well as those I do;' and she gave a squeeze to Joan's arm, through which her own was threaded.

'Ain't her got purty ways?' said one of the girls admiringly to another. 'I wonder what Adam thinks of her?' and, turning, she said to Joan, 'Has her seed Adam yet?'

Joan nodded her head.

'Wall, what does he think of her?'

'I don't think he's had any opportunity of giving his opinion,' laughed Eve, relieving Joan from the necessity of answering what she thought must be an embarrassing question.

'Awh, bless 'ee,' returned the girl, 'you don't want Adam to spake; 'tis actions is louder than words with he, and no mistake. Where's he to-night, then, Joan?

Zekiel told me they wasn't manin' to land 'fore mornin'.'

'Gone up to leave word to Killigarth, I reckon,' said Joan. 'There don't seem much goin' on here,' she added, looking round with a disappointed expression. ''Tis a proper dead-and-alive set-out, surely.'

'Oh no, Joan. Why, I was thinking what a change, and wondering wherever all the people had come from.'

'Oh, 'tisn't nothin' now. You should see it sometimes—the place is like a fair. There's fiddlin' and dancin', and wrastlin', and all sorts goin' on; you can't hear yourself spake for the noise. Now there ain't so much as a fight to look at.'

'The boats was in so late,' said Ann Lisbeth, ' there's scarce bin time to hear of it yet awhiles. 'Twill be better in an hour's time.'

'Supposing we went for a walk till then,' put in Eve.

'Would 'ee like it?' asked Joan, anxious that Eve should be amused.

'Far better than anything else.'

'All right, then; we'll go. Ann Lisbeth, you'll come too?'

And joining arms, the three were about to turn towards the Talland side, when they were met by the old woman who had spoken to them in the morning.

'Hullo, Poll! Why, where be you bound for?' said Joan.

'Who be you?' exclaimed the woman, in her gruff, harsh voice. 'What, Joan Hocken, is it?' and seizing Joan by the shoulder, she peered into her face. 'Here,' she added, apparently satisfied, and letting go her hold. 'What's this they'm tellin' up 'bout Jerrem, as has bin left behind? 'Tain't true that *that* Adam started without un a purpose, eh?'

'I don't know that 'twas a purpose,' said Joan. 'But Jerrem knowed the time o' startin' same as t'others did; and when the time was up, and no Jerrem, why, they comed without un. But 'tain't likely Adam 'd got more to do with it than others had.'

'They that can swaller such words as they needn't fear that lies 'ull choke em,' returned Poll, contemptuously. 'Why, now, you knaws better than to say if Adam hadn't bin so willed, either wan aboard the *Lottery* ha' durst to lave the boy behind. But 'twill come home to un yet; he'll try on his masterful ways too often. And mind this, Joan Hocken——' But Joan had turned aside.

'I don't want to hear no more o' your talk,' she said snappishly. 'I b'lieve you've bin drinkin'; that's what 'tis.'

'Where *to*, then?' retorted old Poll, fiercely. 'Who's to bring a poor ole sawl like me a drap o' liquor, 'ceptin' tis Jerrem? and he left behind, what promised that this time I should ha' tay and brandy too, and was a-bringing it, like he allays does.'

'Oh, well, I dare say Adam 'll find somethin' for 'ee,' said Joan.

'Sommut for me!' exclaimed Poll; 'curses and oaths, that's all I ever gets from he. Lord! but I pays un they back agen,' she added, brightening up at the recollection of her powers. 'I can sarce so well as ever he can. Drinkin', is it, I've bin?' and her voice changed into a whine. 'Wait till you'm up seventy-four, Joan Hocken, and see then if you bain't glad o' a mouthful o' sperrits to keep life in yer insides; but want I may 'fore any but Jerrem 'ud think to trate me; and he a left, too!'

'There, come long, do!' exclaimed the impetuous Joan. 'Now, what'll 'ee have? I'll stand treat for it, so say the word; what's it to be?'

'Why, now, will 'ee, sure 'nuff? Awh, but you'm a dear sawl, Joan Hocken, that you be; and you shall have a baw so handsome as he's lucky, and so I tell 'ee.' And talking as she went, she turned a little to the right, leading the way towards a small public-house, with a hanging-board announcing it to be the sign of the Three Pilchards, which was lighted up in certain anticipation of an increased run of business.

'Now, don't 'ee hinder we,' exclaimed

Poll, in remonstrance to some men gathered near, one of whom laid familiarly hold of Ann Lisbeth. 'Us is a-goin' in here to have a drap o' drink together.'

'One word for us and two for herself,' laughed Joan. 'There, get along in and have what you're a mind to, Poll. I'm goin' to stand treat,' she said, in explanation.

'Noa, I dawn't like that way o' doin' it at all,' said Poll, trying to expostulate by her gestures more than her words. 'Waal, woan't wan of 'ee come? You come, my dear,' she said, catching hold of Eve. 'Iss now, do 'ee, 'cos I knawed yer feyther.'

'No, no,' said Joan, decisively; 'let Eve be. We'se goin' for a walk, and 'twill be too late if we stop. Besides, you ain't in no hurry—stop, to be sure, and you'll get somethin' more gived to 'ee.'

'Only hark to her,' exclaimed old Poll, well pleased at the cheering prospect. 'Awh, 'tis a thousand pities I bain't a han'som' young sailor chap, I'd see if Joan Hocken should go begging for a husban'; but Lord, nowadays men's such a poor lot, with no more sperrit in 'em than a Portygee. I'm main glad I had my time afore any sich was born.'

This last speech set them all laughing, in the midst of which the girls turned to cross the bridge, so as to get by the Warren to the cliff. As they passed by the houses they received several invitations to 'step in a bit,' to all of which Joan answered, 'later on they would, but now they were goin' for a little walk.'

'There's a goodish lot gone by,' said one

woman, who was standing at her door; 'I don't know whether 'tis wrastlin' or fightin' they'm up to, sommat or 'nother's goin' on there; anyways Rawes Climo's in it.'

'Oh, my dear life! here, Joan, let's come on!' exclaimed Ann Lisbeth, who took a very lively interest in the movements of Mr. Rawes Climo.

'But if it's a fight,' said Eve, 'hadn't we best go back?'

'Why for, then? So long as they fights fair I'd so soon see 'em fight as wrastle, wouldn't you, Joan?'

'Depends 'pon who 'tis,' said Joan, philosophically. ''Tain't no fight, Eve,' she continued; 'and wrastlin's only play, you know.'

Thus encouraged, Eve proceeded on towards a crowd which they now caught sight of, assembled together on a small flat space of ground not far off from the building-yard.

The moon was at its full, and its light made all around easily discerned. Joan first ducked her body to try and get a peep between the taller people's legs, then she gave a jump to see if she could catch a glimpse of anything over their heads; and both these endeavours proving futile, she announced it as her opinion that if they didn't try and elbow in they might as well have stayed at home.

Ann Lisbeth was by no means loth to use the necessary exertions, and the three soon found themselves—in considerable advance of the outer circle—pausing to take breath before they attempted a further passage of arms with a formidable-looking opponent in the shape of a thick sturdy girl standing in front of them.

'Who's t'other one?' asked Joan.

'A Looe chap,' returned the girl; 'I ha'n't a heerd what he's called, but he might so well ha' stopped home, he's a bin thrawed twice afore, and now all the sense is knacked out of 'im, and he lies bleedin' like a bullock.'

'Oh dear!' cried Eve, but the exclamation was quite lost on her two companions, whose fresh-whetted curiosity urged them to more vigorous efforts; so that while they pressed forward Eve found little difficulty in slipping her arms from under theirs, and turning her exertions in an opposite direction, she soon found herself outside again, and free to follow her own desires.

She did not wish to go back without Joan, and it was not pleasant to stand loitering on the outskirts of a crowd, so she determined to walk a little distance on along the cliff.

A knot of men, sitting and standing about a rough seat hollowed in the rock, determined her upon taking the lower path, and, without looking in their direction, she walked on, her pace gradually slackening as she got beyond fear of observation.

How calm and still the water looked! Eve was just beginning to drink of the fulness of this new phase of its beauty, when a voice behind her said:

'Cousin Eve, is that you?'

'Oh, Cousin Adam!' and her tone and face showed that his presence was by no means unwelcome.

'Why, how is it you're all by yourself? Where's Joan got to that you're alone?'

'Oh, she's not very far off. We were both together till just this minute. There's a fight or something goin' on, and she's just stopped to look at it. Somebody said one of them was bleeding, and that was enough for me. I didn't wait to see any more.'

Adam laughed.

'Why, you're never such a coward as to be afraid of a drop of blood?' he said. 'Not you!'

'Indeed, but I am. If anybody but cuts their finger I feel faint.'

'That's nice stuff to make a sailor's wife out of,' said Adam.

'I'm not going to be a sailor's wife,' returned Eve, promptly.

'Oh, indeed! how do you know that? I s'pose some of your fine London chaps have stolen a march upon us. Never mind; we'll manage to give 'em the go-by. All's fair in love and war, you know.'

'I don't in the least know what you mean,' said Eve, trying to assume a very indifferent tone. 'But I've no doubt Joan will be looking for me by this time, so I'd best go back.'

'I wouldn't advise you to,' said Adam, standing so that without pushing she could not well pass him. ''Twon't be over for a good half-hour yet, take my word for it; and Joan won't come away till it's ended. There's plenty of time to walk to the end twice over before you'll catch sight of her; that is, if you've a mind to go.'

'Oh, I want to go very much,' replied Eve; 'but there's no need for me to take you,' she added demurely. 'I don't mind a bit going by myself.'

'All right, then; I'll go back,' said Adam.

'Yes, do.'

But the words did not come out very readily, for Eve had certainly not expected to be taken literally. Before she had time to turn, Adam had burst into a laugh.

'So that's the way the London dandies treats the maidens, is it? Well, they're a nice lot to choose from, instead of a good, honest sailor chap, who'd live and die for ye. Now, you take my advice, Cousin Eve: send him a mitten; give him "turmits," as they say hereabouts, and leave it to me to find somebody else to stand in his shoes.'

'You're very kind, upon my word,' said Eve, laughing; 'more like a father than a cousin. But, thanking you all the same, Cousin Adam, when I *am* on the look-out, and that won't be yet awhile, I think I'd as soon choose for myself.'

'All right; so long as he isn't one of

your counter-jumpin', tape-measurin' town fellows, I'll give my consent. But there, I needn't waste words; for I'll bet a guinea, before twelve months is past you won't own you ever saw a man who wasn't a sailor. Why, if you'd bin a man, what would you have bin? Why, a sailor of course, aboard the *Lottery*, eh?'

'And get left behind, like the young man you wouldn't wait for at Guernsey,' said Eve.

But the speech was not out of her mouth before she repented making it, for Adam's face clouded over.

'I only served him right,' he said. 'He's always up to some fool's game or 'nother, which those, who ought to know better, look over, because he's hail fellow with every one he meets. That was all very well years ago, but it doesn't do nowadays; and 'cos I see it, and try to keep things up a little, nothing's bad enough to say of me. 'Tisn't of much use tryin' to alter things while the old man's alive; but if some of them don't learn to spell *obey* before they die, I'm a Dutchman.'

They had by this time reached the projecting flat, and Eve, wishing to turn the conversation into a more pleasant channel, proposed that they should stand for a few minutes and look around them.

'Isn't it most lovely?' she said. 'I didn't think any place in the world could be so beautiful.'

'Yes; 'tis a pretty look-out enough now,' said Adam, 'with the moon shining on the sea like silver, and the stars twinklin' out all over the sky; but, by the Lord! it can put on an ugly face sometimes. I've seen the sea dashing up over where we're standin' now, and the wind drivin' dead on the land, and a surf no vessel could live in. Ah! 'tis time to think o' sayin' your prayers then, for you're within hail of kingdom come, and no mistake.'

'How dreadful!' said Eve, with a shudder, as she conjured up the scene. 'It wouldn't be half as dreadful if the sea looked as it does now. I seem as if I shouldn't hardly mind jumping into it a bit.'

'Shouldn't you?' said Adam, throwing his arm round her waist and impelling her to the brink of the cliff; 's'pose we try it together?'

Eve gave a terrified cry; and drawing her back, Adam said, in a soothing tone:

'Why, what a little coward it is, to be sure! Did you think I meant to throw you over?'

'Of course I didn't,' said Eve, recovering herself; 'it was only because I was startled. I shouldn't have minded else. I should like to look over.'

'Come along, then; I'll hold you tight enough;' and he allowed Eve to bend forward so that she could see the gleaming surf as it rippled and lapped the rocks below.

Eve gave a sigh of satisfaction.

'I feel,' she said, 'as if I could stand like this for ever.'

'So do I,' said Adam.

'I don't want to go indoors.'

'Neither do I.'

'Nor to speak or say a word.'

'No.'

'Only to look, and look, and look!'

And her voice died away with the last word, and she seemed to abandon herself to the full enjoyment of the scene before her. It was one which might well absorb every thought. The vast unbroken mirror of waters, over which the moon flung the great mantle of her light—the fleecy floating clouds—the tall dark cliffs, behind which lay shadowed the little town. At another time Eve would have had neither eyes, nor ears, nor thoughts for anything but this; but now, overpowering these surroundings came a tremulous emotion from within; a something new, which was sweeter than pleasure and keener than pain; which made her long to speak, and yet dread to break the silence. Another moment passed; the spell grew stronger. Then a warm breath stirred the air close to her cheek, and, with a sudden effort, Eve gave a dexterous movement which freed her from Adam's arm, and placed her at a little distance from his side.

'It's quite time we went back,' she said, in an altered voice. 'Joan must have been wondering, for ever so long, where I've got to.'

'The wonder is you ain't at the bottom of the cliff,' said Adam, surlily. 'The next time you think o' being so nimble, I'd advise you to choose some safer place than here.'

## CHAPTER IX.

EVE and Adam walked back in comparative silence. The fight was over; the crowd dispersed; and as neither of them displayed any wish to join the revelry which, on and about the quay, was now in full-swing, they took their way home by a different road.

Eve was vexed and angry with herself—unduly so, she thought—for she could not help losing Joan, neither could she help Adam following her; and as for the rest, she did not know what else she could have done. It was all Adam's fault. She wished he would leave her to herself. She could see they should never agree, and the sooner he found out that she wasn't going to let him take such free ways with her, the better friends they'd be.

As for Adam, he looked the picture of ill-humour, and the expression on his handsome face was anything but a pleasant one; and his thoughts, taking, as they did, the form of a volley of expletives, were the more bitter and lasting because he could not give free vent and expression to them.

The house reached, he pushed open the door, saying, as he let Eve pass in:

'I told you Joan wouldn't put herself out. There she is.'

And there, as he said, dimly discernible through a cloud of smoke, in the midst of several men, sat Joan, before her a glass of a smoking compound, a large bowl of which occupied the place of honour on the table.

'Oh! so you've come at last!' she said, as Eve entered.

'Yes. Didn't you wonder what had become of me, Joan? I was so afraid you'd be frightened to think where I'd got to.'

'Not I,' said Joan, recklessly; 'when I got out they told me where you was gone, and that Adam had gone after 'ee.'

'Oh! then why didn't you come, too?' said Eve, in an aggrieved tone; 'I hadn't gone but a very little way.'

''Cos two's company and three's trumpery, my dear; ain't it, Adam? You'd ha' told me so if she hadn't; that's the best o' bein' cousins, you can speak your mind so free.'

'There, where be goin' to sot to, my dear?' interrupted Uncle Zebedee, feeling, according to his expression, that there was a screw loose somewhere; 'here, bide a bits here,' and he pulled her down on his knee. 'Messmates,' he said, 'this is my poor brother Andrew's daughter, comed a' the ways fro' London to live wi' her old uncle, and keep that raskil Joan in order. What do 'ee say to drinkin' her good health and a welcome home to her, eh?'

Without replying, the company filled their glasses, and, one of them giving the signal by nodding his head towards Eve, the rest followed his example, took a good drink, and then, to signify their unqualified assent to a remark by their leader, that he wouldn't mind 'a foo more o' her sort bein' shipped to this port,' rapped their pipe-stems vigorously on the table.

'Now 'tis your turn to make a speech,' said Uncle Zebedee.

'Her wants to wet her whistle first,' said the weather-beaten old fellow nearest to her, judging Eve's hesitation by the own cause which alone could influence his loquacity. 'Here, Joan, get a glass for her.'

'No, no, Joan, don't! I'll——'

'Take a drap out o' mine,' he interrupted gallantly, pushing his jorum of grog in front of her. 'Doan't fear to take a good pull. I'm a moderate man mysel'; I never exceeds the wan glass.'

'That's true,' replied a sour-faced man with one eye; 'only, somehows, you manages not to see the bottom o' he while there's a drap standin' in the bottle.'

'Then 'tis we won't go home till mornin' this time,' said Uncle Zebedee heartily, 'for there's lashin's more than's put 'pon table; so at it with a will, my boys, for you may walk a deck-seam after a tub o' such stuff as this is. Come, Adam lad,' he added, turning to his son, 'make a pitch somewheres; can't 'ee find room for un beside o' you, Joan?'

'No, I'd rather have his room than his company,' said Joan, getting up to fetch some more glasses; then, catching Eve's rather wistful gaze following her, she selected one with bright-coloured flowers painted on it, saying, as she set it before her:

'There, that putty one's for you!'

Eve's face brightened at what was evidently intended as a peace-offering. She took the glass, expressing her admiration of it; and, having it in her hand, there was no further good in protesting against its being filled.

''Tis quite a ladies' tipple, this,' said the visitor who was doing the honours of the punch-bowl. 'Here, Joan, my dear, hand over your glass agen. You've only had a thimbleful.'

Joan did as she was desired, and then Eve's neighbour said:

'Come, we ha'n't a had your speech yet, you know.'

'Oh! I can't make a speech,' laughed Eve. 'I—I can only say I'm very much obliged to everybody.'

'Waal, that'll do,' said the old fellow, approvingly; 'I'm not wan for many words myself, I likes a foo here and a foo there, turn and turn about; give all a chance, and pass the grog round—that's what I calls behaviour in good company. Now then, listen to what the maid's got to say,' he said, bringing down his fist on the table, and thereby setting everything on it in a jingle, 'Zebedee's niece is a-goin' to spake.'

Thus signalled out for observation, there was nothing for it but to repeat her former words, and having got out: 'I feel very much obliged to everybody,' Eve turned her blushing face round to her uncle, unaware that Adam was behind, and that he, as well as his father, could see her pretty air of shy embarrassment.

'Hear! hear! Well said!' roared out old Zebedee, reassuringly, giving her cheek at the same time a hearty, sounding kiss while Adam exclaimed, with ill-suppressed irritation:

'Why don't you let her sit down like the rest, father?—there's chairs enough for all, surely;' and he pointed to a vacant chair next to Joan, of which, with a nod to Uncle Zebedee, Eve took possession leaving Adam to seat himself at a little distance off.

Without further remark, Adam plunged into conversation with the guest who happened to be his neighbour; Eve entered into an explanation with Joan; and the rest of the company returned to their grog and pipes, and the repetition of their oft-told tales of privateering, press-gang adventures, and escapes from French prisons. Eve's interest had just been aroused by one of these narratives, when Joan, noting that her glass remained untouched, pushed it significantly towards her. Eve waited for an instant, and then pushed it back again;

but Joan would not be denied, and they were still engaged in this pantomime when Adam, who had apparently been watching them, said dictatorially:

'Let be, Joan! Why do you press, if she don't want to drink it?'

Thinking he was annoyed at her non-compliance, Eve said:

'Yes; I'm sure it's very good, but I'm not used to such things. I don't know that I ever tasted spirits in my life.'

'Well, taste that, then,' said Adam.

She shook her head.

'Do,' said Adam, entreatingly. 'To oblige me, put your lips to it.'

'Oh, well, I don't mind doing that,' said Eve, raising the glass to her mouth.

'Now,' he said, turning it so as to drink from the same place, 'I'll finish it for you;' but before he could carry out his intention,

Joan, whose face had suddenly blazed up with colour, knocked the glass out of his hand, and before he had time to recover his surprise, her own and its contents were shyed to the other end of the room.

'I say, what's the row there?' exclaimed Uncle Zebedee. 'Why, Joan, what's come to 'ee maid, that you're smashin' up the glasses? 'tis reyther early for that sort o' game yet awhiles.'

'Best to take a drap more,' said the distributer of the punch. 'There's no coor like a hair o' the dog that bit 'ee.'

''Tisn't nothin' but a bit o' skylarkin', uncle,' said Joan, ashamed of her outburst of temper. 'You ain't offended, Eve, are you?'

'No, I'm not offended,' said Eve, who sat aghast and dumbfoundered at such reckless breakage.

'I haven't angered you, Adam, have I?' said poor Joan, humbly.

'Certainly not,' said Adam, coldly. 'If you haven't angered Eve, you haven't angered me. You've broke two glasses, that's all.'

'Oh, darn the glasses!' said Zebedee, who saw there was some antagonism between the two. 'You'm welcome to break all the glasses in the house, if it plases 'ee—only let's have pace and quietness, and sommut to drink out of.'

'Suppose somebody gives us a song,' said Zekiel Johns. 'Here, Joan,' he added, by way of throwing oil on the troubled waters, 'come, strike up "Polly Oliver"—us ha'n't a had she for a brave bit.'

Joan felt in little mood for singing, but after causing this temporary disturbance, some amends for it was due from her; so without more delay than was occasioned by the request that she would not begin until pipes and glasses were made ready for undisturbed enjoyment, she commenced. The tune, though not unmusical, was somewhat monotonous — a defect compensated for by the dramatic pathos of the narrative, and Eve was soon completely engrossed in the fortunes of the girl who, in order to follow her lover, had donned male attire.

'Now Polly being sleepy, her hung down her head,
And asked for a candle to light her to bed,'

sang Joan, when open flew the door, and on its threshold stood a tall gaunt figure, whose sudden appearance seemed to strike consternation into all present. Glasses were overturned, pipes thrown down. Some of the men sprang to their feet—all was instant confusion.

'What news, Jonathan?' hastily exclaimed Adam, who had advanced to meet the new-comer. 'Where are ye come from?'

'Liskeard,' answered the man. 'I was 'bliged to give 'em the double by comin' that ways. Word's passed along that you be looked for with a fine rin o' goods.'

'H'm, I thought us was safe this time, anyhow,' exclaimed Zebedee. 'Now, how did they come to know that, I wonder?'

'But they can't tell that we're in yet, surely?' said one of the men.

'Noa; they'm thinkin' you'll make the land sometime to-morrow. The cruiser's to get under weigh 'bout daybreak, and the sodgers is to come on here and be ready for 'ee ashore.'

'Then there's no time to be lost,' said Adam, decisively. 'We must land as soon as we can, and after that make ourselves scarce.'

Some more talking ensued, during which hats were found, lanterns produced and trimmed, and then the two girls and Jonathan were left alone.

'They ain't going to sea again, are they?' Eve ventured to ask.

'Not yet awhile,' said Joan; 'they've got somethin' to do to the boats first. But you must go off to your bed, Eve. You ain't used to sittin' up late.'

'No; let me keep you company, Joan. I'd rather do that than go to bed,' pleaded Eve.

Joan hesitated.

'I think best not this time,' she said. 'I fancy uncle 'ud rather you was to bed when he comes back agen ; and Jonathan 'll be here, you know. You ain't going yet awhiles, I s'pose, Jonathan ?

'Noa, not I. I wants sommat to ate, I does. Got any mate-pasties or that put by, Joan Hocken ? 'tis no good hidin' things frae me.'

'Here, you haven't spoke to my cousin yet ?' said Joan, laughing.

'What, *she?*' said Jonathan, who had drawn a chair to the fire, over which he sat cowering. 'What's her called ? I've a seed she somewhere's afore. I don't like her looks at all, I doesn't.'

'There, that ain't no way mannerly,' said Joan, intimating by a look towards Eve, and a tap on her forehead, that Jonathan was weak in the head.

'Has her got any money ?' he asked, suddenly turning round.

'I don't know,' said Joan. 'You have though, haven't ye?'

'A bag full!' exclaimed Jonathan. 'Gowlden guineas! and half-guineas and crowns!' he added, with an unction that showed that the very mention of their names was a positive enjoyment to him.

'No pound-notes for you, Jonathan, eh!' said Joan.

'No, I b'lieve 'ee,' chuckled Jonathan. 'They dosn't dare to give me sich.'

'Now you'm goin' to tell me where you keep 'em all to, this time?' said Joan, trying by her banter to keep him quiet, until she and Eve had set the room a little straight.

Jonathan shook his head.

'I shan't tell 'ee nothin', not while her's here,' he said, jerking his elbow in Eve's direction. 'Her'd go and blab, and be the ruin o' us all, her would. Can't 'ee send her home, Joan?'

'Don't take no notice of un,' Joan said in an undertone. 'He ain't got his wits about un like me, so he says just what comes into his head. I'll soon stop his mouth, though;' and she went into the kitchen and lifted down the best part of a large pie. 'Now what else is there?' she said reflectively, 'for when he sets to, that won't go far. His head can't stand drink— it drives un mad,' she added in explanation to Eve's look of amazement, 'so he makes it up with vittals; and if he could ate the same meal twice over in every house in the village, he'd be welcome, for the good service he does us all.'

Eve only waited until Jonathan's meal was spread before him, and then, yielding to a further entreaty from Joan, she rather reluctantly went off to bed; half induced by Joan's assurance that she intended very soon to follow.

'I shall only wait till they've had all they want,' she called out, 'and then I shall come too, Eve.'

Eve determined that though she went to bed, she would not go to sleep, a resolution which she kept for fully ten minutes after her head was on her pillow, and which she was not certain she had for more than a few moments broken when, some hours later, she started up to find Joan's place beside her still vacant. I must have been sleeping, she thought, and then, as consciousness returned, she began to feel that, instead of a doze, her sleep had been one of some duration. She sat up and listened: not a sound could she hear. The room was dark, the house quite still. A feeling of undefined fright took possession of her. Surely Joan had not gone out; they would never leave her in the house alone. What was to be done? She had no light, and no means of getting one, for those were the days of tinder-boxes and brimstone matches, and with even these appliances, few, save the prudent housewife, provided themselves against emergencies.

Growing desperate, Eve slipped out of bed, and listened with sharpened attention. Not a sound save that which came from the clocks, whose measured tick, tick, seemed mocking the nervous thumping of her heart.

Something must be done—she could not go back to bed again; so, groping about, she found her gown, and then her cloak, and hastily throwing these on, she cautiously crept down the stairs to the door which opened on the sitting-room. There was evidently a light, for its glimmer came through the chinks of the door. Timidly she laid her fingers on the latch; it lifted, but she pushed in vain. The door would not yield; it was bolted on the outside. Pausing to recover this surprise, Eve braced up her trembling courage, and then she turned and remounted the stairs, her heart no longer fluttering, and most of her fears ousted from their place by a sudden determination to find out the reason of this mystery.

Leading from her bedroom was another door and a passage from which stairs led down to the kitchen below. Along by this way Eve crept. To her amazement the kitchen, though empty of people, was nearly filled with furniture, between the various articles of which she stepped her way, and then catching full sight of the room beyond, she paused. Surely no! that wasn't the place she had been sitting in?—bare and stripped of everything. Why the very walls were gone, and in their place, arranged one above another, stood rows of small barrels. The floor was strewed with ropes and tools, the fire was out, and candles flared in the wind which came in at the half-open hatch of the door.

Eve stood bewildered, not knowing whether to go forward or back; but another instant decided her, for in front of the hearthstone, close by where, on the previous night, she had sat, emerging from below, a head slowly appeared, and another glance showed her that the face was the face of Uncle Zebedee. Eve caught her breath. This then must be smuggling, and without further thought she turned, flew up the stairs, jumped into bed, and hid her head under the clothes.

With returning calmness, however, came the recollection, that if Joan came up, the dress and cloak would betray her; so she got up and put them back into their place, and then again lay down to listen and wait—not long—before the noise assured her the furniture was being replaced. Then, after an interval, came a buzz of voices, but not until a faint glimmer of grey had crept into the room did Eve hear the bolt undone, footsteps ascending the stairs, and Joan coming stealthily in. Involuntarily Eve shut her eyes, nor though Joan seemed to have brought over a candle to look at her, did she open them, determining that while Joan was engaged in undressing she would pretend to be aroused, and awaken. But there was no opportunity afforded for the carrying out of this deception, for Joan having satisfied herself concerning her companion, merely set down the candle, blew it out, and threw herself, dressed as she was, on the bed.

## CHAPTER X.

THE sun was streaming into the window when Eve awoke with a sudden confused recollection of something having happened. She started to find Joan sitting on the edge of the bed, rubbing her half-open eyes.

'Why, Joan,' she exclaimed, 'whatever time can it be? And do you know how you went to sleep last night? You never undressed yourself.'

'No,' said Joan, drowsily, 'I know I

didn't. What with one thing and 'nother, I couldn't get the rids of 'em till ever so late, and then I was so tired I'd no heart to take my things off.'

'Look at your nice gown,' said Eve, vexed that the pretty chintz should present such a bedraggled appearance.

'Iss, I s'pects 'tis in a proper cram,' returned Joan; 'but there, I can't help it. I must put on something else, I s'pose.'

'Oh, I'll soon iron it out for you,' said Eve; 'so let's make haste and get our breakfast over. I s'pose uncle and Cousin Adam have gone?'

Joan by a nod of her head intimated that they had.

'What, to Guernsey again?' asked Eve.

'To Guernsey! no,' said Joan: 'not

near so far. They'll be home again to-morrow, or maybe next day.'

'But what made them go so sudden?'

'Well,' said Joan, 'I don't know that you'd be much the wiser if I was to tell 'ee, Eve; still, I don't see how you're to bide here without some word bein' said. Uncle was for trustin' 'ee altogether, only Adam wouldn't have it. He said 'twas enough for you that they was gone out pilotin'. Now you know, Eve, I'm measurin' you by my own bushel, and I know such talk wouldn't take me in, more partickler as I've got to ask 'ee to tell anybody that comes that you've never cast eyes on 'em.'

'Adam must think I'm silly,' said Eve, indignantly.

'I don't know what he thinks,' replied Joan. 'I only know I ain't goin' to follow out his biddin' without seein' the reason for it, no more than anybody else's; besides, there's nothin' that I see to hide from 'ee, nor to be ashamed to tell 'ee of. What uncle brings he buys and pays honest money for, and if there's a risk in bringin' it, why he takes that risk; and if that isn't havin' a right to keep it if he can, why I don't know nothin' about it, that's all.'

'But what is it that he does bring?' said Eve.

'Why, sperrits to be sure. 'Tis like this: they says, "Here, you must pay dooty." "No," uncle says, "I won't—I'll bring it dooty free." Well, he does so, and if he can land it safe, well and good; 'tis his to sell or to drink, or to do what he likes with. But if the excise gets scent of it, down they come and tries to seize it all, and if they do seize it, 'tis gone, and so's the lives of any they catches with it. So no blame to 'em, if they'm took hard, when each man knows the bit o' hemp's ben growed to make the rope his neck's to swing by.'

'Oh, Joan!' exclaimed Eve, 'not hung! you don't mean that they'd hang them!'

'Iss, but they would. They hanged ole Israel Jago. 'Twas long afore any o' our times, but uncle minds it. His feyther—why your grandfeyther, then—was one o' they who went up to London with Israel's wife to try if they couldn't get un off; but 'twasn't o' no good.'

'What did his poor wife do?' said Eve, sympathetically. 'Wasn't she in a dreadful way?'

'Well, I don't know,' laughed Joan; 'they do say her stayed waitin' outside the gaol-doors all night, and in the mornin', 'stead o' biddin' un a last farewell, as they all thought her'd comed to do, her pushes into his hand a red cotton handkercher. "There," her says, "take thickee and gie me thuckee, for sure thee doesn't want a silk neckercher to be hanged in."'

'What a dreadful woman, Joan!'

'No, her wasn't—her didn't leave no stone unturned to get un off; but, as her said, her knew then 'twas no more good; so what call was there to waste more than had bin 'pon un?'

'Well,' said Eve gravely, 'I'd rather live on dry bread and water, Joan, than have any one get their living in such a way as that. Why, I should never know a minute's peace. Each time they went away I should never expect to see them again.'

'So you think,' laughed Joan, 'but you'll very soon get over that, and make as sure of their bein' back as if they was comin' by the mail-coach. Oh, it doesn't do to be fainty-hearted about anything! What is to be will be, I say, so there's no need to run out to meet trouble on the road. But, remember,' she added, changing her voice to a graver tone, 'you've a part to act to-day, Eve; and if the sodgers comes to search, you must carry on with them, as if there wasn't such a thing as a keg to be found for twenty miles around.'

'But is there any hidden near here?' asked Eve, determined to test how far Joan's confidence would extend.

'Come 'long down with me,' said Joan, 'and I'll show 'ee. Now, you see these walls,' she continued, after they had reached the sitting-room, which was rearranged in the same order in which Eve had first seen it. 'Well, the sides here and there are hollow, and will open behind this,' and she pointed to a recess in which stood a chest. 'There's a hidin'-place, and there's another underneath the floor. They're all full o' liquor now, but when they'm empty again you shall see 'em. I'll get uncle to show 'em to 'ee, for it takes more than my strength to get 'em open.'

Eve smiled. Turning, she took hold of Joan's hand.

'No need for that,' she said. 'I've seen them already.'

'You have!' exclaimed Joan. 'Why, when?'

'Last night.' And Eve related her adventures, and how in her fright she had had her curiosity satisfied.

'Well, I never did!' said Joan, in amazement; 'only to think now, if I hadn't told 'ee, what a sly one you'd ha' took me for!'

'No, I don't know that—but I am glad you trusted me, Joan. I don't think anybody need ever fear to do that.'

'So I knew when I told 'ee,' said Joan, promptly; 'and though I listened to what Adam said, I made up my mind all the time to follo' out my own mind. Women knows one another a deal better than the men ever finds 'em out, and right they should to.'

'I shan't forget Mr. Adam's opinion of me for one while,' said Eve, huffily. 'I am sure I ought to be very much obliged to him for thinking so ill of his own cousin.'

'I don't know that I ever saw un think quite so much of any one before,' answered Joan, looking wistfully at her. 'Oh!'

she exclaimed passionately, biting her lips, and drawing in her breath, 'I'd forgive anybody who'd make him mad in love, so that he'd no hold over hisself, but just showed what a fool he was, whether one or twenty stood by.'

'Hasn't he ever cared for anybody, then?' asked Eve.

'Not he,' said Joan; 'there ain't ne'er a one in Polperro good 'nuf for un. There's they you'll hear tell up, that Adam said this and told 'em the other; but what if he did? He hadn't got no manein' in it, and so they oft to know by this time.'

'Then I don't think he has any right to act so,' said Eve, pleased to make a hole of the slightest flaw in Adam's conduct. 'I haven't much opinion of those who try to mislead others. Everybody ought to say what they mean, and mean what they say.'

The earnestness with which this sentiment was delivered seemed to amuse Joan, and, beginning to laugh, she said:

'I shall set you to talk to Jerrem when he comes back. 'Tis he's the raskil with all the maidens 'bout here; and that minds me. Eve, 'bout that letter you said you'd write. Will 'ee do it some time to-day?'

'Yes, of course I will, if you'll tell me what uncle wants to say.'

'Well, uncle thinks 'tis best it came from me like, warnin' un not to take no notice, 'cos nothin' more than a trick was meant, and sayin' he's not to stop loiterin' there, but to come across back home to wance in anythin' he can get passage in. And,' she added, after a minute's reflection, 'to soften it down a bit, you might say that we're all well—and that you'm here, and have wrote the letter. That'll do, won't it?'

'Capitally,' said Eve; 'the best way will be for me to write out what you've said as I think, and then when it's done, read it out loud to you.'

This plan meeting with Joan's approval, Eve sat down, and as soon as the necessary materials were supplied, commenced the epistle, which she worded as though it came from Joan. This pleased Joan mightily, and she stood leaning over Eve, watching her fold up the letter, and direct it to Jeremiah Christmas, at Louis Reinolds's, Guernsey.

'Now you shall seal it yourself,' said Eve, when all else was completed.

'Well then, I must look for my thimble,' said Joan, delighted that some portion of the performance was to be really her own, ''cos I haven't got no seal.'

'Oh, but I have,' said Eve; 'I'll run and fetch it.'

The seal was one which had hung on a watch that Reuben May had taken in exchange. It was of little value, but the old French motto, *Amour avec loiaulté*, had struck Reuben, and he had begged Eve to accept it.

The circumstance of its being wanted brought the donor to Eve's mind, and as she turned over her small hoard of treasures, seeking it, her conscience smote her for her forgetfulness of her friend. Since the morning after her arrival she could not remember having cast a single thought in his direction. These were not the days of universal letter-writing, so that though Eve had promised to send Reuben a letter, and tell him how she found herself among her new relations, she did not intend, neither did he expect her, to write this until she was thoroughly settled down. Still, she had never thought fresh faces could have so completely driven him from her mind, and she was trying to find some excuse for her apparent heartlessness, when there came a sudden clatter of horses' hoofs.

'Eve, they'm here! the sodgers! Come down!' called out Joan, hurriedly.

Eve ran down with a scared face.

'Oh, Joan! What am I to say?'

'Why, nothin'; seem as indifferent as you can. I didn't talk about it a purpose, 'cos you shouldn't go workin' yourself up. Just seem to take it all off-hand, and as if you thought it like their impidence to come anigh the place;' and the sound drawing close to, she caught up the towel she had a little time before laid down, and went on with her employment of washing the breakfast-things. Another minute, and the rap of something heavy sounded against the door.

'Come in!' cried Joan.

Rap, rap, rap! sounded more vigorously.

'Come in!' repeated Joan, in a louder tone.

'Sha'n't you open the door?' whispered Eve.

Joan was going to shake her head, but just at this moment the hatch was flung open, and a man's voice said:

'I don't know whether you want me to come into your house horse and all, young woman?' taking it for granted by the voice that the speaker was a woman, and a young woman.

'I don't want neither you nor your hoss,' returned Joan; 'so if you'm waitin' for a welcome from me, you'm both like to take root in the place where you be.'

'Ah, I see; you know what we're after.'

'Glad to hear I'm so sharp,' retorted Joan. 'I s'pose they've told 'ee 'twas a complaint that's catchin', that you'm all come peltin' down here alongs.'

'We've come to catch something that it's no use your hiding, Mrs. Pert,' laughed the man, a good-looking sergeant; 'and we've a warrant to search the house in the King's name.'

''Tis very much to his Majesty's credit to be so curious about such humble folks,' said Joan, with a look of saucy defiance. 'P'rhaps you'll ask un' to send word next time, then we'll be a little better prepared for 'ee.'

'Oh!' laughed the man, 'we take things as we find them; so pray, ladies, don't disturb yourselves on our account.'

'Oh! are they going upstairs?' exclaimed

Eve, starting up, as the party having entered and divided, one of them opened the door which led to her room. 'My! and I've left my workbox open, and the things all about.'

'Well, go up with 'em,' said Joan. 'I don't know what they'm here for, but I s'pose 'tain't to demand our scissors and thimbles.'

'I should be very sorry to demand anything but a kiss from two such pretty lassies,' said the sergeant, who had remained in the room, bestowing a look of most undisguised admiration on Eve.

'If you'll come upstairs with me,' he added, addressing her, 'you'll see that nothing of yours shall be touched.'

At a glance from Joan, Eve rose up to go; and then remembering that the letter lay on the table, she reached back to take it up, but the soldier's quick eye had anticipated her.

'Allow me,' he said, catching it from under her hand, and reading the direction: '"Jeremiah Christmas—Louis Reinold's—Guernsey." Oh! so Jeremiah's at Guernsey is he? I've got a friend going there, and he'll be proud to take this for you;' and he made as if about to put the letter into his pocket.

Eve held out her hand.

'Give it back to me,' she said; 'there's things in it,' she added shyly, 'I shouldn't care for anybody else to see.'

'All the more reason why I should take care of it,' replied the young man; only too well pleased to detain anything which might afford an opportunity of feeding the admiration the sight of Eve had filled him with.

'No, but it isn't anything to do with anybody here.'

'Why, is it a love-letter then? and is Jeremiah your sweetheart?'

'Don't answer him, Eve,' exclaimed Joan, with pretended indignation. 'Let it go—I would; 'twon't take 'ee much trouble to write another. Far rather that, than spend words on such as think they'm doin' a fine mornin's work, to try and cower two lorn maidens whilst their men's all out o' the way.'

'Oh no, they're not,' said the sergeant, with a derisive smile. 'We shall come upon the men presently, hiding under the straw, or in the cupboards, or up the chimney, stored away with the kegs.'

'Why, now, if somebody musu't ha' split 'pon 'em,' said Joan, with a gesture of mock fear.

'Here! Dick, Bill, Tom!' she cried, 'do 'ee come 'long down; the sodgers is sent to sweep the chimleys, my dears.'

'I don't think you can be one of this place,' said the soldier, seeming to take no heed of Joan's banter. 'You haven't got such a saucy tongue as most of the young women about here. Where might you come from?'

'From London,' answered Eve, hoping to propitiate her interlocutor. 'I have only been here a week.'

'And how many sweethearts have you got in that time?'

'Not any—there hasn't been any to have. Besides, if there had, I——' and hesitating, she cast a wistful glance at the letter, exclaiming, 'Oh, do give it to me!' with such an irresistible look of entreaty, that the sergeant held the letter towards her, saying:

'I don't know that I've any right to keep it, though before I give it up I must know the name of its pretty owner. What are you called?'

'My name is Eve.'

'Eve,' he repeated dubiously.

'Iss, and my name's Timersome,' called out Joan. 'Come, I knaw'd you was dyin' to knaw what I be called, only you'm too sheep-faced to ax the question.'

'I'll tell you what it is—' he began, but at that moment the soldier from upstairs came down, and, without waiting to conclude his speech, he turned hastily round, saying to Eve: 'Now I am going upstairs, so will you come and look after this work-box?'

Joan made a movement to let them pass, and Eve, taking the hint, followed the sergeant upstairs. The plan of search seemed to be arranged so that while a certain number of the party were told off for the actual hunting about, the remainder were left to guard the rooms and the various exits and entrances of the house. In order that each one should stand his chance of discovery and be free from all suspicion of bribery and connivance, the men constantly changed posts, and so it happened that all had to run the gauntlet of Miss Joan's cutting remarks and sharp speeches; but they had a soldierly weakness for a saucy tongue with a pretty face, and took all she had so complaisantly, that a strict disciplinarian might have accused them of a decided lack of zeal in the performance of their duty. For want of knowing what else they could do, they stamped on the boards of the floors, opened the cupboards, pushed about the chairs and tables, made dives in and under the beds, and then, wondering if they were not there, where on earth they could be, began and did the very same thing over and over again.

In their hearts they wished the runners rather than themselves were set after this sort of game. It was not the business they cared to be up to, and would only turn all the people against them; which would not be so pleasant, seeing that not a landlord in Fowey, Looe, or Liskeard ever kept a score against a soldier. However, it would not do to be too lenient in their bearing; so, to keep up appearances, each fresh comer knocked about the things, flung open the doors, and made grand discoveries of heaps of straw which turned out to be stored apples, and mysterious barrels which proved only salted pilchards.

The same thing, with slight variations, was gone through in each house they entered; until about one o'clock the sergeant decided it was of no use remaining longer. The goods were not to be found, the men had evidently not landed, and they had best get back to Fowey, and leave the revenue cruiser the glory of a capture.

Joan, with her elbows leaned on the door-hatch, stood watching the little party take their departure.

'Wish 'ee well, if you'm goin',' she called out saucily.

'Oh, don't break your heart about us, young woman,' replied one of the men. 'We shall be back again soon; 'twon't be long before you have the pleasure of our company again, so keep yer spirits up.'

'Thank 'ee,' said Joan; 'what sperrits us

has got, us generally try's to keep, though 'tis a hard matter agen such a knowin' set as you sodgers be.'

'Ah, you're a saucy wench,' laughed the sergeant, who had by this time ridden up. 'I won't have nothing to say to you, but I must say good-bye to my pretty friend Eve. Where has she hidden herself to, eh?' and stooping, he tried to catch sight of her; but Eve only drew herself farther back, and the horse beginning to grow fidgetty, the young fellow had to ride away without having accomplished his wish.

'There, let's run out and have a last look at 'em,' cried Joan. 'Good riddance to bad rummage!' she called out.

At the sound of her voice the soldier turned and flung back an answer; but he had gone too far, the words could not reach them.

'I can't tell what 'tis he's sayin' of,' laughed Joan, her spirits rising as the sound of the retreating hoofs grew fainter. ''Twas somethin' 'bout you I reckon, Eve,' she added, as they turned back into the house; 'and hadn't he got somethin' held up in his hand a-dangling of? Whatever could it be, I wonder?'

## CHAPTER XI.

FOR some time after the soldiers had taken their departure all was bustle and excitement. Neighbours ran in and out of each other's houses, telling and hearing of narrow escapes and many adventures. Friends laughed and joked over their thoughtlessness or their discretion; here a stray keg had been dropped into the pig's bucket, there one caught up and popped under the baby in the cradle. Every one grew bolder, their usual recklessness gaining strength as they saw how little they had to fear from such a set of Johnnie Raws as the unlucky searchers were universally voted.

'Well, now 'tis most time to think o' dinner,' exclaimed Joan, sitting down almost exhausted with chattering and laughing.

'Oh, don't let's bother about getting dinner for us two,' said Eve.

'All right,' replied Joan; 'we'll just take what's to hand, and then we'll put on our things and go up alongs. I want to see how Ann Lisbeth's folks have got on; they'd got more stowed away than we have.'

'But don't they never find any of it?' asked Eve.

'Not in the houses, they never have. Back 'longs in the summer there was a pretty good find in the standin' corn near Landaviddy, but though they seized the kegs they couldn't tell who'd put 'em there.'

Eve gave a shake of her head. 'I can't bring my mind to think it's exactly right,' she said. 'I wish uncle had nothing to do with it. Couldn't he give it up if he liked?'

'He could, so far as money goes,' answered Joan; 'but Lord! he never will, and I don't see neither why he should. Everybody must get their livin' one way or 'nother; and as he often says, 'tis child's play now compared to the war-time. Then you never did know when you'd see 'em again. What with bein' pressed into the king's ships, and taken off to French prisons, 'twas a terrible time of it.'

'Has uncle ever been in prison?' asked Eve.

'I should think he had, and never expected to get out agen neither; but they managed it, and he and three others broke out one night and got clear off. And 'twould make your blood run cold to hear of all they went through—how they'd to lie all day long hid away in the ditches, half dead with hunger and cold; then as soon as night came they'd push on, though where to; they couldn't tell, only 'twas towards the sea.

'But how ever did they live through?' said Eve. 'Had they got any money with them?'

'Not a penny piece; and if they had, 'twouldn't ha' been o' any use, for they couldn't spake the tongue, and durstn't ha' gone anighst a shop, 'cos o' bein' knawed as prisoners o' war wherever they shawed their faces.'

'How did they manage, then?'

'Well, uncle says to this day 'tis more than he can tell; but manage they did, and to reach the watter-side too; and then they watched and watched, and at last a boat comes in sight, with a young French chap rowin' his sweetheart, and making for the shore. Well, they lands; and then, by what uncle could make out, the maid persuaded the young man to see her a bit on her way home. So he looks round, and seeing the coast clear and nobody nigh, he hauls up the boat, stows away the oars, and off they goes; and then 'twas oh, be joyful! and no mistake, with th' other poor sawls. They didn't take long afore they was out o' their hiding-place, afloat, and clean out o' sight o' land and everybody 'pon it; and there they was tossin' about for I can't tell 'ee how long, and had given up all for lost, and made sure to the bottom of the say they must all go, when all to wauce a vessel hove in sight, and after a bit picked 'em up; and somehow the capen—though 'twas a French privateer—was got over to land 'em at Jersey, and from there they got on to Plymouth, and so comed back safe and sound after all.'

'Oh!' exclaimed Eve, 'after one escape like that, I'd never have gone to sea again —never!'

'Lor' bless 'ee, iss, you would,' said Joan, decidedly. 'Why, only see what a muddlin' life 'tis for a man to be stoppin' ashore week in and week out. He grows up a reg'lar cake, like that Sammy Tucker o' ourn, one side half baked and t'other forgot to be turned. Here, I say, Eve,' she exclaimed, with sudden emphasis, 'us'll have to go up and see mother agen, or else the place won't hold her. I wonder her hasn't bin down before now; her's generally putty nimble when anythin' o' this sort's goin' on.'

'She doesn't approve of it at all, does she?' said Eve.

'So she says,' returned Joan.

'But why should you think she says what she doesn't mean, Joan?'

'Because she don't act consistent—no more don't none of 'em up there. Mother's very high and mighty in her talk 'gainst smuggled goods and free-tradin', but she'd be in a nice quondary if she didn't get her tea cheap, and her sperrits for next to nothin'; and after arguin' with me for the whole afternoon 'pon the sin and wickedness o' such ways, her'll say, " Mind, Joan, the next lot o' chaney uncle gets I wants a match to my plates, an' you can set a bowl or so aside for me to look at." '

'What, does uncle bring china too?' said Eve.

'Not exactly bring it,' said Joan, 'but he often gets it out o' the homeward-bound Injiamen and ships comin' up Channel. They'm glad enough to get rids of it before the Custom-house gentry catches sight of it. There was some talk of their getting somethin' this time. I wish they may, then we should come in for pickin's.'

Eve smiled.

'Why, what should I do with china?' she said.

'Oh, but 'tisn't only chaney. There's chintz, and silk, and crape shawls, and lots of beautiful things. We'd find 'ee somethin' you'd know what to do with: 'sides, you ain't always goin' to wear black, you know; and some o' the chintzes is sweet and pretty, sure 'nuf.'

'I shan't leave off my black for many a long day to come, if ever,' said Eve, gravely. 'Why,' she added, smiling, 'I shouldn't know myself for the same in such finery as you wear, Joan.'

'Oh, wait a bit,' said Joan, significantly. 'Time 'ull tell. We shall see what we shall see.'

'No,' returned Eve, resolutely; 'you'll never see any difference in me. I ain't one to change. What you see me to-day you'll find me to-morrow.'

The necessity for going into the kitchen to seek what remained for this substitute for dinner created a diversion in the conversation. Some minutes elapsed, and then Joan reappeared, laden with the remnants of a squab-pie, some potted conger, and a couple of good-sized apple-pasties.

'There, this 'll do,' she said, setting the dishes down on the table which Eve had made ready. 'I don't want much, do you?'

'No; I could have gone till tea-time,' said Eve.

'Oh, I think us 'll have our tea out some place, 'twill make a change; and there's lots has asked me to bring 'ee.'

This decided, they sat down to their meal, laughing and chatting with that unflagging loquacity which is natural to young girls with light hearts and unclouded spirits. The events of the morning were still naturally uppermost in their minds, and Joan commenced rallying Eve on the evident impression she had made on the young sergeant.

'I never thought he'd ha' given 'ee the letter agen,' she said. 'Oh my! I did have a turn when I seed it in his hand.'

'So had I!' said Eve. 'I made certain he was going to put it in his pocket.'

'So he was, till you give him that innicent look;' and Joan tried, by casting down her eyes and raising them again, to give a comical imitation. 'Lord,' she laughed, 'I wish to goodness I could do it! Wouldn't I gammon 'em all!'

'But I didn't mean nothing particular,' protested Eve. 'I only looked up quite natural.'

'Natural or no, it melted his heart, or whatever sodgers has got in the room of it.'

'I think you're all too hard on the poor soldiers,' said Eve. 'If they do come searching, 'tisn't on their own account; 'tis only because it's their duty.'

'Oh, well then, let 'em take their duty some place else, laughed Joan; 'for in Polperro 'tis sperrits dooty free, and men free o' dooty.'

'I think the men certainly make free enough,' said Eve.

'Why, how?' returned Joan. 'You haven't hardly seen any of 'em yet, 'ceptin',' she added, after a pause, ''tis Adam. Was it he you was meanin', Eve?'

Eve blushed.

'Oh, I don't know that I meant him in particular, though I do think he makes much more free than he need to.'

'In what way? Do 'ee mean by offerin' to kiss 'ee?'

'Well, yes.'

'But you let un when you two was out together last night?' said Joan, half questioningly.

'No, indeed I didn't,' replied Eve, decidedly.

'What, didn't he try to?' continued Joan.

'Whatever he may have tried he didn't get,' said Eve, the colour heightening on her face.

'Well, I never did!' exclaimed Joan. 'I wouldn't ha' believed any maid alive could ha' baffled Adam!'

'Why not?' and Eve assumed an expression of great surprise. 'Can't you refuse him what you don't want to give him?'

'Oh!' said Joan, with laughing bitterness, 'I'm his cousin, my dear. He don't ask nothin' o' me — what he wants he takes.'

'I'm his cousin too,' said Eve, setting her mouth firmly, 'but he'll never do that with me.'

'Awh, don't you make too sure o' that,' said Joan. 'Others ha' thought the same afore now, but Adam's proved one too many for 'em.'

'You speak as if everybody must give way to Adam,' exclaimed Eve. 'Why, Joan, quite as good men as Adam have been forced into falling in love, and with no hope of having it returned neither.'

'Iss, but had they got his ways?' said Joan, doubtfully. 'If so, I've never met none of 'em.'

'Nonsense,' said Eve, contemptuously. 'Why, you told me yourself that most of the girls cared for Jerrem more than they did for Adam, and by your manner I thought so did you.'

'Well, I b'lieve I do sometimes, only that—but there!' she cried, breaking off impatiently, ''tis o' no use talkin' nor tryin' to show the why nor wherefores, but unless I'm very much mistook, 'fore you're many months older you'll find it out for yourself.'

Eve gave a confident shake of her head. 'If your head don't ache, Joan, till you see me running to Mr. Adam's beck and call, you'll be pretty free from pain, I can tell you. I'm not at all one to be taken by a man's courting; and if I had been, you and me would never have met, for up to the last minute of my coming away somebody was begging and praying, and all but going on their knees to me to keep me in London.'

'And you wouldn't stay?' said Joan, immediately interested in the confidence.

Eve shook her head.

'Didn't 'ee care for un then? Was that the reason of it?'

'Oh, I cared for him, and I care for him

now; and don't think, for goodness and kindness to me, I shall ever meet his fellow anywhere. But somehow I couldn't love him, and the more he strove, the more shut against him I seemed to get.'

'H'm!' said Joan, with surprised perplexity; 'still I don't see, 'cos you couldn't like he, that that's to hinder 'ee from caring for Adam. Wan thing is certain, though,' she added, 'there's no fear if you shuts yourself against he, of his striving over much. The boot's on the other leg with Adam.'

Eve laughed. 'There's no need of our wasting words on talking about what's so little like to happen; and if we're going out, I think 'tis time to go. So I'll run up and put on my things; shall I?'

'Yes, do,' said Joan; adding, as Eve was turning from the table: 'Was the wan who wanted 'ee to stop in

London, he you was telling me about before—Reuben May—eh, Eve?'

'Oh, you mustn't ask no more questions,' said Eve; 'I'm not going to give any names.'

'Come, you might so well,' said Joan, coaxingly. 'I shouldn't tell nobody, and I always have a sort o' feelin' for they that places their love at the wrong door.'

'To be left till called for,' laughed Eve, saucily.

'Oh, I can see that you're a hard-hearted one,' said Joan, as she pushed back her chair and rose from her seat. 'I only wish,' she sighed, 'that I could be the same. I b'lieve things would ha' gone ever so much smoother than they have.'

'Well, I haven't asked any questions,' said Eve, 'and I don't mean to, either. I shall wait till Jerrem comes home, and I see you and him and Adam together; then, I suppose, it won't take long to tell who is Mr. Right.'

'I don't know that,' laughed Joan. 'Wan thing is certain, 'twill putty soon be known who is Mr. Wrong—there'll be no mistakin' that. But that minds me 'bout the letter; don't let's forget to take un with us, and on our way. I'll give it to Watty Cox, to take with'n to Looe to-morrow. We didn't put the seal to it, did we?'

'No. I'd just gone up for it;' and Eve felt in her pocket, and then began looking among the things on the table.

'What be looking for?' asked Joan; 'there's the wax and the candle.'

'I'm looking for the seal,' said Eve. 'I know I brought it down with me.'

'Isn't it in your pocket? You didn't

show it to me. I never saw you with it.'

'I'd just got it in my hand when you called upstairs,' said Eve; 'and I remember I didn't wait even to put back the till of the box. I jumped up off my knees and ran down, and I'd got it in my hand then.'

'Well, p'rhaps you took it up agen. Run up and see.'

Eve ran up, but in a few minutes she returned with the little box in her hand.

'I've turned everything upside down, and taken the things out one by one,' she said, beginning to repeat the fruitless operation, 'but there's no sign of the seal. Besides, I feel certain, now, that I laid it down 'pon the table.'

'Lord!' exclaimed Joan, giving vent to a fear that had crossed both their minds, 'that impident rascal of a sodger has never taken it, to be sure? But don't 'ee know, I told 'ee I saw un danglin' a somethin' in his hand.'

'Oh, Joan!'

'My dear, depend on it that's where 'tis gone—so you may make your mind easy, then. For goodness gracious' sake, don't 'ee tell Adam; he'd vow we'd bin up to some games with un, and the very sight of a sodger's coat drives un as mad as a bull.'

'Oh, bother, Adam!' said Eve, in a vexed tone; ''tis losing the seal I care for. I wouldn't have parted with it for anything.'

'Why, was it a keepsake from your poor mother?'

'No, not from her, but from a friend. I valued it very much.'

'Did he give it to 'ee, Eve?'

'I don't know who you mean by he,' said

Eve, refusing to accept Joan's evident meaning; 'but there's no secret as to the giver. 'Twas given me by the only friend'—and she laid unnecessary stress on the word—'I had in London.'

'Reuben May,' put in Joan, filling up the slight pause which Eve had made.

'Yes, Reuben May. 'Twas he gave it to me.'

'Was it his first gift?' asked Joan.

'His first and his last,' said Eve, smiling. 'You forget that people there haven't got money to be so free with as they have here, Joan. Reuben was like mother and me, had to work for every penny he spent.'

'What's his trade, then?'

'A watch and clock maker,' said Eve, with becoming pride; 'and very clever he is at it too. Mother always said if Reuben couldn't make anything go, 'twas no use anybody else trying. But there, he's the same with everything,' added Eve, distance holding a magnifying-glass over Reuben's oft-despised superiority. 'His reading's like listening to a sermon, and his writing's beautiful and like print, 'tis so easy to read; and as for knowing about things, I don't believe you could ask him a single question but he'd find an answer for it.'

'And yet with all that you couldn't bring your mind to care for un. No, now'—and Joan held up her hands to drive away all denial—''tis o' no manner o' use your sayin' "No," for I'm as certain that 'tis Reuben May you was speakin' of as if you was both standin' before me together.'

'Oh, well, if that's the case, there's no more good in me speaking,' said Eve.

'Not a bit,' answered Joan. 'If you was to talk till to-morrow, I should only think the same. Now, ain't I right?' she said, throwing back her head and looking at Eve with smiling entreaty.

'I'm not going to say "Yes."'

'Well, but you won't say "No,"' persisted Joan.

Eve turned away.

'Ah!' cried Joan, clapping her hands, 'I knew I was right, from the moment you spoke his name. I felt a sort o' drawin' towards un, so p'r'aps, after all, things'll come right between 'ee.'

'They're quite as right as I want them to be,' said Eve, decisively.

'Oh, of course. When the love's all t'other side, 'tis wonderful how contented folks can be. As for he, poor sawl, I dare say his heart's too heavy for his body. Well, if it'll do un any good, he's got my pity—and seemingly my luck too,' she added, with a sigh. 'But here, come 'long—let's finish the letter, and as we haven't got a seal, we'll make shift with a thimble. There!' and she surveyed the blot of red wax with eminent satisfaction—'that'll make it safe. Stop, though, I must drop a kiss,' and down fell the wax again. 'That's from me. Now, to make it fitty both sides alike, there's one from you.'

'Oh, you silly thing!' exclaimed Eve. 'You forget I don't know him, and he doesn't know me.'

'Well, s'pose he don't, what o' that? 'Twill taste the sweeter. 'Sides, I shall tell 'un that anyways he's got the start o' Adam there, and had the first kiss after all.'

'I declare I won't wait another moment,' exclaimed Eve, with feigned impatience. 'If you don't come at once, Joan, I'll go without you. The afternoon will be gone before we've left the house.'

## CHAPTER XII.

JOAN led the way towards Talland Lane, but before turning out of the green they were stopped by a voice calling:

'Joan, Joan Hocken, my dear, do 'ee want anythink to Plymouth or thereabouts?'

'Who is it?' said Joan, turning to catch sight of a comely, middle-aged woman who had just stepped out from one of the neighbouring houses. 'Oh, you, Jochabed?'

'Iss, my dear; I was just comin' your ways, 'cos, if all goes well, us starts by three to-morrow mornin', for we's got a tidy load this time.'

'Who be 'ee goin' to, then?' asked Joan.

Jochabed cast a look of inquiry towards Eve, which Joan answered by saying:

'All right, 'tis Uncle Zebedee's brother Andrew's daughter.'

'Is it, sure? Ah I heerd her'd acome. And how do 'ee find yerself, my dear?' she said, turning to Eve.

'Very well, thank you.'

'Her likes the place, then?'

'Yes,' answered Joan, 'though what with wan thing and t'other, us has bin all in a uproar since her's been here.'

'Ah, sure!' said the woman; 'what a how-de-do they gentry kicked up this mornin'! I see 'em into your house makin' more free than welcome.'

'Iss, that they did, and no mistake,' laughed Joan.

'And what for ever they comes I can't think,' continued Jochabed, 'for they allays goes back the same, neither wiser nor heavier. I wish to goodness they dratted excise men would learn a lesson from the same book.'

'Nonsense! you ain't 'feared o' any o' they,' said Joan; 'why, you and Aunt Catarin 'ud take the shine out o' a dozen men o' they sorts.'

'No, no, now, I dawn't say that,' laughed Jochabed, who had a particularly musical voice; 'and I'm sure, whatever folks says, they as knaws me best can testify that 'tain't in me to lay a finger's weight on man, woman, nor cheeld, 'less I'm fo'ced to it.  And I was never more for pace and quietness than that very mornin' when us met a party, who shall be nameless, on Battern Cleaves; and more than that, up to the last I holds in his hand a little passel that I keeps by me done up for anything suddent-like.  But no, he woudn't let his fingers close 'pon it.  Now, I says, don't 'ee go standin' like the mayor o' Market Jew, in your own light; but words were lost 'pon un.  Have it he would, and have it he did; and they *says* he never stirred in his bed for days, which I can well credit, for my poor arms ached sore if his body didn't.'

'There's a Trojan for 'ee, Eve!' exclaimed Joan, tapping Jochabed on the arm; 'that's somethin' like bein' able to take yer own part, isn't it, for a woman to give a man—an excise man, mind 'ee—

such a drubbin' that he's 'shamed to report he met her, and for fear it should get wind never informed against her, though he saw the sperrit—didn't he, Jochabed?'

'Lor' bless 'ee, iss, my dear; what was to hinder un? when the skins was busted so that they dripped 'till the liquor ran like waster? then that soaked through to the tay, and that gived way. You niver in all yer days saw such a set out as 'twas, and I was a regular object, too, but nothin' to he, poor sawl! Waal, I did feel for un, that's the truth; a man looks so foolish to be mawled by a woman, and his face a sclumbed all over—but whatever could I do? As I said to un, my childern's mouths must be filled so well as yourn; but 'tis no use to stop and bandy words with a man who thinks he's no need to take "No" for an answer. But there, I'm keepin' you, my dears, and myself too,' she added apologetically.

'No, you ain't,' said Joan; 'we'm only goin' so far as Ann Lisbeth's, and then down to Talland Bay, and back home by cliff for Eve to look at the say. Her's mazed 'bout the say,' she added, in an amused tone.

'Well I never! Whether she be or no,' and Jochabed regarded Eve with increased interest "'tis a bootiful sight, surely; and though I was born and reared by it as you may say, I was never tired o' lookin' at it, 'ceptin' 'twas when my baw, as was a man-o'-war's-man, was outward-bound; then I used to wish there'd never bin no say made.'

'Then your husband is a sailor?' said Eve, by way of making a remark.

'Wa-al no, not exactly, my dear; he's a

sawyer—or, to speak more proper, he was. But he ain't nothin' now, dear sawl; he's in hebben, I hopes—a good dale better off than any o' we. Iss, for the dropsy took un off like the snuff of a candle, and he was gone in three weeks; that's twenty years agone. When I married un, you might ha' took a lease o' his life—not that I minded that then, for I didn't valley un not the snap o' my finger. My heart was set 'pon the man I told 'ee of.'

'And how was it you didn't marry him, then?' asked Eve.

'Why, so I meant to; but as he was comin' from Fowey—for my folks lived to Lansallos then—out jumps a gang o' press-men and carr's un óff then and there. And if 't hadn't bin for Joshuay Balls, us shouldn't niver ha' knawed for years what had comed of un; but it happened Joshuay was crooked down behind a hedge, and saw all of it from beginnin' to endin'. Awh, when they told me, I was like anybody mazed, I was, and no wonder neither, for there was my furniture got, and my clothes ready, down to the very ring—iss, same wan I's got 'pon my finger now, and no man. Howsomedever, I hadn't got long to wait for he, for the very next Monday, as that was on the Friday, up comes Sylvester Giles—he'd bin casting sheep's-eyes that way afore—and talks me over; so that 'fore the week was out I gived in, and let un stand in t'other man's shoes. Ah, take my word for 't,' she added, with an assured nod of her head, ' that, so far as wedlock goes, what is to be will be; for marriages is made in hebben, and can't be marred on earth; and the right Jack 'ull have his Jill, though 't 'as gone so far, as another man buyin' for hisself the ring t'other two's to be wedded with.'

'Lors, I wonder whether any man's abought the ring that 'ull marry me, then?' laughed Joan.

'There's a plenty 'ud be proud, and happy too, if so be you have 'em to buy 'ee wan, for each o' your ten fingers,' said Jochabed, admiringly, 'and no blame to 'em, neither; for, says Solomon the Wise, "A good wife's a good prize;" and, if they comes to me for a character, I'll tell 'em they'll search the place round for fifty miles and more, but they wun't find two Joan Hockens. And the longer you knaws her, my dear,' she said, turning to Eve, 'the stronger you'll love her.'

'I feel sure of that,' replied Eve, taking the hand which Jochabed held out, for they had by this time reached a gateway into which she was about to turn.

'You ha'n't got a bit the look o' the maidens hereabouts,' continued Jochabed; 'and yet her face don't seem strange. Her's like somebody I's a knawed. Who is it, Joan?'

'I can't tell,' said Joan, 'less 'tis Adam you 'm thinkin' of.'

'You've a said it—that's who 'tis,' said Jochabed, decisively. 'Wa-al, my dear, 'tain't speakin' ill o' nobody's face to feature 'em with Adam, is it? Only I says to you as I says to he, booty's only skin deep, and han'som' is as han'som' does.'

During these last words Jochabed had opened the gate and gone through; she now only waited to say, 'Then you can't mind nothin' you want this time?' and to hear Joan's answer before she turned down a narrow path leading to a field, at the farther end of which was an opening by which she could reach her cottage.

'How far is Plymouth?' asked Eve, as the two girls stood watching Jochabed's retreating figure.

'Twenty miles or so.'

'And will she walk all that way?' asked Eve.

'Yes. Oh! 'tain't nothin' much of a walk that,' said Joan; 'only she'll carry four skins o' sperrit and a good dollup o' tea.'

'Skins of spirit? Why not put it in a bottle?'

''Cos she carries it all about her,' replied Joan. 'You couldn't sling a parcel o' bottles about 'ee.'

'Oh! then doesn't she have a basket?'

'Why no, unless 'tis to put some

trumpery in she makes out to be sellin' o'; 'cos she don't want nobody to know what she's carryin', and they that buys from her buys on the sly. 'Tis all under the same flag, my dear, free trade and no dooty; but come on, we're close to Ann Lisbeth's now, though 'tis ten to one if we finds her at home, we've took such a time in comin'.'

True enough, when they reached the cottage they found Mrs. Johns (Ann Lisbeth's mother, an invalid, and through rheumatism constantly confined indoors) alone. Ann Lisbeth had left an hour before, to do some errands. She had gone down the steps by Mrs. Martin's house, through to the Warren, and by this means the friends had missed each other.

'How's she comin' back?' asked Joan.

Mrs. Johns did not well know; Ann Lisbeth had told her not to wait tea, as most like she should stop and take hers at her cousin's, Polly Taprail's.'

'Oh! all right then,' said Joan; 'we're goin' there, so we shall all meet;' and after a little more gossip about the adventures of the morning, and how fortunate it was that they had not cleaned up the place, so that the littering mess the soldiers made, tramping over everything, was not of any consequence, the two girls took their departure, and continued their walk up the steep lane, stopping every now and again to pick a few of the blackberries which hung in tempting profusion. Above these stood bushes covered with scarlet hips, in and out of which twined the honeysuckle with just here and there a late blossom standing sickly-looking and alone; these and the long trails of briony, gay with ruddy berries, proved sore temptations to Eve, who lagged behind, gathering here and there, while Joan carried on her steady plunder of the blackberries.

'There,' she cried at length, 'if I go on like this I shan't be able to eat a bit o' tay; so come on, Eve—do. I say,' she added, picking her way across a tiny stream which spread over the path from a fern-sheltered basin into which a spring came dripping down, 'take care, or our shoes and stockings won't be fit to be looked at.'

'That's a pity for those that wear buckles,' laughed Eve.

'Uncle gave 'em to me,' said Joan, putting her feet together and surveying them with visible satisfaction; 'they're rale silver; they was poor aunt's. He's got another pair put by for Adam's wife, he says. ''Tis much better he gave 'em to you, so I'll tell un.'

'No, no, I don't want them,' said Eve. 'I like to see other people in such things, but I don't care for them at all for myself; besides,' she added, with a touch of resentment rankling towards Adam, 'I should be very sorry to deprive Adam's wife of anything.'

'Nonsense,' laughed Joan. 'Take all you can get; that's my maxim. And as for hoardin' up and layin' by for Adam's wife, who we never saw, and perhaps may never come, is what I call folly, and so I tell uncle. Nobody 'ull thank un for it, and least of all Adam.'

'No, I shouldn't think he was overburdened with gratitude,' said Eve, sarcastically.

'I don't know that,' said Joan; 'but

'tis this with Adam ever since he was born, he's had all he wanted a'most fore he'd asked for it. Nobody's ever gainsayed un in a single thing. Aunt and uncle and my mother, and lots more, think his ditto was never made, 'til I b'lieve he's got it in his head that the world only goes round to please he and his fancies.'

'And yet people don't seem so very fond of him,' said Eve.

'No, they ain't; they're afeard of un, and that's the truth; and in wan way I don't wonder at it neither, for he ain't content that you should know that he's better than yourself, but he must make 'ee feel it somehow.'

'Indeed! I can't see that he's any better than other people,' exclaimed Eve.

'Oh, but he is, though,' said Joan.

'He knows more—is a better scholar, perhaps,' continued Eve; 'but——'

'That ain't all,' interrupted Joan. ''Tis in other things 'sides scholarin'. He don't give way to drinkin; ain't mixed up with no cockfightin', nor fightin' o' no sort; nothin' o' that's any pleasure to he. Then in the sharin', whether their faces or their backs is to un, 'tis all one to Adam; there's yourn, and that's hisn, and no more nor less is made of it.'

'But that's only honest, Joan.'

'Iss, I know that; still he needn't make 'em feel like a pack o' chates, 'cos one or two's a happened now and then not to know t'other from which. He's terrible hard that way; once slip, and down you stay with Adam.'

'Well, I don't like people who deceive and shuffle, myself,' said Eve.

'Ah,' said Joan, 'some's as God made 'em, and t'others as the devil finds 'em; but Adam acts as one who made hisself perfect, and can keep hisself the same.'

'Of course that's going too far,' said Eve. 'Still, I think we've got a great deal in our own hands, you know, Joan, and I have not much patience with people who go wrong, for it always seems to me they might have helped it if they'd tried to. Mother and me used often to argue about that; for no matter how bad any one was, poor dear, she'd always find something to excuse them by.

'But I thought your mother was so religious,' said Joan, with some surprise.

'So she was; but there's nothing against religion in that, Joan, is there?'

'Iss, my dear; 'tis a good deal against the religion I sees carried on here. If you was to ask my mother and they, her'd tell 'ee that o' Sundays, when the chapel-doors was shut, 'tis Glory Hallelujah to they inside, and fire and brimstone to whoever's out; though, somehow, I can't never bring my mind to b'lieve that's what the Bible means it to be.'

'Why, of course not,' said Eve; 'you've only to read for yourself to know that. You've got a Bible, Joan, haven't you?'

'There's wan at home,' said Joan, evasively.

'Is there? Where? I don't think I've seen it.'

'No, you haven't; 'tis kept locked up in the ches n' drawers, 'long o' some o' poor aunt's things. She bought un afore Adam was born, so uncle don't like un read in, 'cos 'twould get thumbed so; the bindin's beautiful, and 'tis as good as new. I don't s'pose it's been opened half-a-dozen times.'

Eve was silent for a few minutes; and just as she was about to renew the conversation they came to a gate, which Joan opened and passed through, saying the path was now so narrow that they would have to walk in single file. This extremely narrow lane opened into a good-sized turnip-field, where Eve's attention was caught by a sight of the old manor-house, with its arched doorways and granite-mullioned windows.

'That's Killigarth,' said Joan. 'Ain't it a ancient old place! How would 'ee like to live there, Eve, eh?'

'I'd rather live down by the sea,' said Eve.

'Would 'ee, sure 'nuf? Awh, but that's a splendid place inside,' continued Joan.

'There's one room big enough to turn a coach-and-four inside, with Adam and Eve, and all of 'em, plastered up on the ceiling; and outside there's a hedge so high, and so broad, that you can walk four abreast a-top of it, out so far as a summer-house overlookin' the sea. There ain't much of the summer-house left now, but the hedge is there all right.'

Such an unusual curiosity naturally occasioned some surprise; and Joan was still endeavouring to give satisfactory answers to Eve's numerous questions concerning it, when they began to descend the steep hill leading down to Talland Bay.

'Ah!' exclaimed Eve, giving vent to a deep-drawn sigh of satisfaction as the sweep of Talland Bay and beach came into sight. 'This is the sort of view I like, Joan; I could stand looking at this for ever.'

'Well, better ask Arbell Thomas to let 'ee live with she. That's her house, down there; do 'ee see, close in by the lime-kilns?'

'And is that the church you go to?'

'Very seldom; whenever any of us goes to church, 'tis to Lansallos; leastwise, that's where we'm bound to go, 'cos we'm in Lansallos parish.'

Eve gave a despairing shrug.

'I shall never understand it,' she said; 'the place is all Polperro, isn't it?'

'Of course it is!'

'Well, but yet you keep on calling it Talland and Lansallos.'

'And for this reason,' said Joan, stooping to rake together four or five loose stones. 'Now, look here, suppose we say these stones is Polperro, now, and she made a division with a clear space between the two heaps; 'this we'll call the brook—that divides two parishes. All this side is Talland, and they must go to Talland church to be married and buried; all that side is Lansallos, and must be married and buried in Lansallos church. Now do 'ee understand?'

Eve went over the explanation to herself; then she said:

'Yes, I think I do understand now.'

'All right, then. Before we go on I want to ask Arbell if she's got any ducks fit for killin', 'cos if so, us'll have a couple.'

'You don't want me for that, do you?' said Eve; 'so, while you go in there, let me wait here—shall I?'

'Very well,' said Joan. 'Then don't come through the gate, 'cos we haven't got time to go no farther, and I won't be a minute or two 'fore I'm back agen.'

So saying, she pushed open the gate, let it swing behind her, and disappeared towards the cottage, leaving Eve to become more familiar with the scene around her. A patchwork of fields spread out and ran down to the cliffs, which sloped towards a point where they overhung the sea, and shadowed the little pebbly beach below. Not a tree was in sight, so that Eve's eyes wandered across the unbroken line of undulating land until they rested on the hillock-raised tower of the old grey church, beneath whose shelter lay the dead, whose plaintive dirge the sea seemed softly singing; and straightway a mist gathered before Eve, and the eyes of her heart looked upon a lonely grave in a far-off city churchyard. Was it possible that little more than a week had passed since she stood bidding farewell to that loved spot? If so, time had no span, but must be measured by the events it chronicled. Only a week! yet her life seemed already bound up in fresh interests, her feelings and sympathies entangled in a host of new doubts and perplexities. Affections hitherto dormant had been aroused, emotions she had not dreamed of quickened. It was as if she had dropped into a place kept vacant for her, the surroundings of which were fast closing in, shutting out all beyond and obscuring all that had gone before; and at this thought the memory of her mother was hugged closer to her heart, while the sight link which bound her to Reuben May seemed turned into a fetter.

'He ought never to have taken such a promise from me,' she said, with all the ungenerousness of one-sided love.

Then, after a few moments' pause, moved

by some impulse, she ran across the green slope which hedged the cliff, and bent over; but the place where on the previous night she had stood with Adam was hidden from view, and turning, she walked slowly back, wondering what could have made her wish to look at that particular spot.

Certainly not any feeling of love she had towards Adam, for the thought that Adam was the one who would not trust her stung her with a sharpness which made the desire for revenge come keen, and the thought of it seem sweet. And out of her vivid imagination she swiftly conjured up an image of Adam, humbled and enslaved; and as she stood still, enjoying her pictured triumph, the click of the gate recalled her wandering senses, and turning round she was met by Joan, who said:

'Let's get back as quick as can, for Arbell says one o' the boats is in; and one o' the Climo's told her that word had come o' somebody havin' seed Jerrem.'

'Oh! then what a pity we sent the letter!'

'Yes; I forgot all about that,' said Joan. 'But never mind, Watty can't have took it yet. So on our way home we'll call and tell un we wants the letter back agen; we needn't say for why, only that we've a changed our minds, and there's no call to send un now.'

END OF VOL. I.

BILLING AND SONS, PRINTERS AND ELECTROTYPERS, GUILDFORD.<br>S. & H.